目次

Level 5-2　Test 1—Test 20

嗨！你今天練習了嗎？

完成一回習題後，你可以在該回次的○打勾並在 _100_ 填寫成績。

一起檢核英文實力吧！

(Level 6 (Test 1—Test 40)、PLUS (Test 1—Test 10) 請見下一頁喔)

英語 Make Me High 系列

108課綱、全民英檢中高級適用

進階 英文字彙力

4501~6000 PLUS⁺ 習題本

丁雍嫻 邢雯桂
盧思嘉 應惠蕙 編著

三民書局

Level 6　Test 1—Test 40

PLUS　Test 1—Test 10

Answer Key

Level 5-2 Test 1

Class: _____   No.: _____   Name: _____   Score: _____

I. 文意字彙 (40%)

_____ 1. When little Johnny saw his father carry a b_____e, he knew his father was going to work.

_____ 2. The e_____r walls of the apartment need washing.

_____ 3. The diligent student is e_____ed to a full scholarship.

_____ 4. The country is ruled by a r_____n government, not by a king.

_____ 5. The gardener t_____med the tree with a pair of garden shears.

II. 字彙配合 (請忽略大小寫) (40%)

(A) scope	(B) porch	(C) pastries	(D) directory	(E) masterpieces

_____ 1. Amelia is good at making _____, especially banana pie.

_____ 2. Let me look up Jane's telephone number in the _____.

_____ 3. In the English class, we were asked to read several literary _____ of the 20th century.

_____ 4. The boy was sitting on the _____ of the house waiting for his father to return.

_____ 5. The boss gave the staff _____ for creativity.

III. 選擇題 (20%)

_____ 1. All the executives were in _____ at Friday's meeting.

    (A) compliment   (B) attendance   (C) scope   (D) porch

_____ 2. The country is undergoing a _____ from monarchy to a republic.

    (A) conversion   (B) masterpiece   (C) narrative   (D) trim

_____ 3. Some voters say that elections are about _____.

    (A) interior   (B) pastry   (C) quota   (D) ideology

_____ 4. The _____ denied all charges against him and pleaded not guilty.

    (A) sibling   (B) verdict   (C) defendant   (D) masterwork

_____ 5. You can see the _____ when light passes through a prism.

    (A) story   (B) directory   (C) spectrum   (D) interval

Level 5-2 Test 2

Class: _____　No.: _____　Name: _____　Score: _____

I. 文意字彙 (40%)

_____ 1. The boy took third place in the race and got a b_____e medal.

_____ 2. When the girl said she was going to tell a story, all of the kids c_____red around her.

_____ 3. A lot of fans s_____ed for tickets for the concert.

_____ 4. The speaker s_____ned up his suit before entering the conference room.

_____ 5. The couple had a f_____s time at the Christmas party.

II. 字彙配合 (請忽略大小寫) (40%)

(A) attic	(B) idiot	(C) resemblance	(D) defied	(E) tripled

_____ 1. It is surprising that the two brothers bear little _____ to each other.

_____ 2. All the toys I played with in my childhood are stored in the _____ now.

_____ 3. You _____! Don't you know you are fooled?

_____ 4. The tourists got into trouble because they openly _____ the law.

_____ 5. We have _____ the profits of the company this year.

III. 選擇題 (20%)

_____ 1. These companies are all regarded as separate _____.

　(A) sieges　　(B) negotiations　　(C) entities　　(D) patches

_____ 2. After an angry argument, it seemed impossible for the couple to _____ up their relationship.

　(A) comply　　(B) patch　　(C) approve　　(D) speculate

_____ 3. People are protesting against military _____ in other countries' affairs.

　(A) disapproval　　(B) mattress　　(C) racism　　(D) intervention

_____ 4. Alice looked _____ in her wedding gown.

　(A) gorgeous　　(B) wonderful　　(C) triple　　(D) idiotic

_____ 5. Dr. Watson is a(n) _____ of alternative medicine.

　(A) convict　　(B) triple　　(C) idiot　　(D) practitioner

Level 5-2 Test 3

Class: _____ No.: _____ Name: _____ Score: _____

I. 文意字彙 (40%)

_____ 1. I take it for g_____ted that children should respect their parents.

_____ 2. You must get a p_____t for your invention so that no one else can copy it without your permission.

_____ 3. After being scolded by his mom, Tom s_____med the door in her face.

_____ 4. The village's population is largely c_____ed of factory workers.

_____ 5. All the students agree to n____e Susie as the student representative.

II. 字彙配合 (請忽略大小寫) (40%)

(A) sphere	(B) illusion	(C) therapist	(D) meantime	(E) investigator

_____ 1. A(n) _____ is an idea that is untrue or mistaken.

_____ 2. A(n) _____ is responsible for carrying out investigations.

_____ 3. A(n) _____ is an object that is round in shape like a ball.

_____ 4. The lady is a speech _____, helping children who have difficulty in speaking properly.

_____ 5. Our plane will depart one hour from now, and in the _____ we can shop around in the duty free stores.

III. 選擇題 (20%)

_____ 1. The _____ strongly advised his client to remain silent in court.

(A) therapist (B) attorney (C) predator (D) entrepreneur

_____ 2. This flagpole is not completely _____ to the ground.

(A) resident (B) coherent (C) obvious (D) vertical

_____ 3. The _____ of this book deals with the history of Brazil.

(A) bulk (B) correlation (C) faculty (D) meantime

_____ 4. Our fishing boat was _____ on the reef.

(A) scrapped (B) racked (C) stranded (D) disclosed

_____ 5. The badminton player finally won a _____ in the tournament.

(A) delegate (B) lawyer (C) sphere (D) trophy

Level 5-2 Test 4

Class: _____ No.: _____ Name: _____ Score: _____

I. 文意字彙 (40%)

_____ 1. The musician has been f____d by classical music since childhood.

_____ 2. The t____n fees of universities have been raised recently.

_____ 3. Two genuine paintings of Van Gogh were put up for a____n.

_____ 4. Sam's essay is full of i____y and sarcasm.

_____ 5. The burglar d____ted the alarm system and then broke into the house.

II. 字彙配合 (請忽略大小寫) (40%)

(A) slot	(B) envious	(C) pathetic	(D) corridor	(E) bureaucracy

_____ 1. The two boys stopped fighting as the teacher suddenly appeared at the end of the _____.

_____ 2. I have to deal with the school's _____ if I want to change courses.

_____ 3. Having lost all his money in gambling, the man is now caught in a very _____ situation.

_____ 4. Many girls are _____ of Natalie's beautiful face and perfect figure.

_____ 5. Insert some coins into the _____, push the button and then you will get the drink.

III. 選擇題 (20%)

_____ 1. Jack and Jill met again by _____.

(A) backbone   (B) nomination   (C) coincidence   (D) bureaucracy

_____ 2. The trade agreement will have far-reaching _____ for our future.

(A) slots   (B) delegations   (C) implications   (D) scripts

_____ 3. The poor man injured his _____ in a street fight.

(A) spine   (B) radiation   (C) mentor   (D) nomination

_____ 4. Saudi Arabia is one of the _____ producers of oil.

(A) premier   (B) envious   (C) compulsory   (D) residential

_____ 5. The _____ of the Korean War was awarded a medal.

(A) radiation   (B) veteran   (C) gravity   (D) corridor

Level 5-2 Test 5

Class: _____ No.: _____ Name: _____ Score: _____

I. 文意字彙 (40%)

_____ 1. Don't i_____e in self-pity. It's useless to feel sorry for yourself all the time.

_____ 2. The drunk man s_____hed the bottle into pieces.

_____ 3. This student did not s_____t his essay on time.

_____ 4. During the air r_____d, people stayed in the shelters.

_____ 5. The lady divorced her husband for his g_____d for wealth.

II. 字彙配合 (請忽略大小寫) (40%)

(A) tumor	(B) butcher	(C) journalism	(D) authorized	(E) conceded

_____ 1. My mom often buys meat from that _____ because the meat he sells is quite fresh.

_____ 2. The president _____ the ambassador to negotiate with the U.S. yesterday.

_____ 3. Patrick finally _____ that it was his mistake.

_____ 4. The doctor is performing an operation to remove a(n) _____ from the patient's brain.

_____ 5. Elijah resolved to go into _____, hoping that he could thus raise public awareness of many important social issues.

III. 選擇題 (20%)

_____ 1. This wealthy lady is well-known as a _____ of the arts.

(A) thesis   (B) patron   (C) butcher   (D) respondent

_____ 2. The two paths _____ into one under an oak tree.

(A) merge   (B) concede   (C) patronize   (D) envision

_____ 3. The video is popular and attracts many _____.

(A) tumors   (B) sectors   (C) premises   (D) viewers

_____ 4. The angry people managed to overthrow the _____ government.

(A) intentional   (B) authorized   (C) deliberate   (D) corrupt

_____ 5. Many celebrities attended the dinner party, including several Nobel _____.

(A) customers   (B) collaborations   (C) nominees   (D) discourses

Level 5-2 Test 6

Class: _____ No.: _____ Name: _____ Score: _____

I. 文意字彙 (40%)

_____ 1. The spy c_____ed a plan to steal the file.

_____ 2. A d_____t is a person who has firm belief in democracy.

_____ 3. The movie was shown from the v_____t of a little boy.

_____ 4. The couple decided to move from the m_____n area to the suburbs to avoid the noise and busy traffic.

_____ 5. The school bell is ringing. Please r_____e your seats.

II. 字彙配合 (請忽略大小寫) (40%)

(A) smog	(B) episode	(C) rallied	(D) grieved	(E) notified

_____ 1. The development of the Internet is an important _____ in the history of technology.

_____ 2. Mr. Cannon has _____ for his dead wife for years.

_____ 3. The old man had trouble breathing because of the terrible _____ in the city.

_____ 4. All the members must be _____ of any changes in the program.

_____ 5. One week before the election, many people _____ to the support of the candidate.

III. 選擇題 (20%)

_____ 1. Some parents are quite liberal and give their children considerable _____.

    (A) notification   (B) tuna   (C) autonomy   (D) smog

_____ 2. It is _____ that our lives will end one day.

    (A) judicial   (B) inevitable   (C) fiscal   (D) collective

_____ 3. At my request, Mr. White brought his _____ to the party.

    (A) spouse   (B) subsidy   (C) corruption   (D) canal

_____ 4. The monthly _____ for our health insurance went up again.

    (A) episodes   (B) premiums   (C) thighs   (D) seminars

_____ 5. Demonstrators stormed the building and _____ the meeting.

    (A) grieved   (B) pedaled   (C) disrupted   (D) notified

Level 5-2 Test 7

Class: _____ No.: _____ Name: _____ Score: _____

I. 文意字彙 (40%)

_____ 1. Following the doctor's advice, Susan uses a m_____l amount of salt in her food.

_____ 2. I prefer to g_____l sausages rather than steam them.

_____ 3. The suggested r_____l price of the lamp is $10 each, but if you buy a dozen, I can give you a wholesale price.

_____ 4. The dish was too sour. The cook probably added too much v_____r.

_____ 5. Peter decided to apply for the job because of the s_____l salary.

II. 字彙配合 (請忽略大小寫) (40%)

(A) snatched	(B) counseled	(C) uncovered	(D) squad	(E) notion

_____ 1. My doctor _____ me to exercise regularly to relieve my pressure.

_____ 2. I have no _____ of what will be waiting for me behind the door.

_____ 3. Put your bag under the arm lest it be _____.

_____ 4. The building had been evacuated before the bomb _____ arrived.

_____ 5. A plot against the president was _____ by some FBI agents.

III. 選擇題 (20%)

_____ 1. The priest believes in Catholic _____.

    (A) inequity   (B) doctrine   (C) counsel   (D) denial

_____ 2. My sister worked part-time on a _____ during the winter vacation.

    (A) canvas   (B) senator   (C) jug   (D) ranch

_____ 3. Competition is a(n) _____ part of their culture.

    (A) uncovered   (B) pedestrian   (C) inherent   (D) fleeting

_____ 4. Get lost! You shall never cross the _____ of this building again!

    (A) collector   (B) notion   (C) threshold   (D) conception

_____ 5. The doctor _____ medicine for the patient's headache after diagnosis.

    (A) prescribed   (B) barbecued   (C) ranched   (D) snatched

Level 5-2 Test 8

Class: _____ No.: _____ Name: _____ Score: _____

I. 文意字彙 (40%)

_____ 1. The soldier stood e_____t when saluting the general.

_____ 2. You need to renew your v_____a before it expires.

_____ 3. More d_____y evidence was found to prove Paul's fraud.

_____ 4. Make sure your meals contain all the n_____ts that are necessary for good health.

_____ 5. You must g_____p the rope tightly. It's the only thing that can save your life.

II. 字彙配合 (請忽略大小寫) (40%)

(A) jury	(B) carnival	(C) squashed	(D) inherited	(E) condemned

_____ 1. During the _____, there was a big parade, and thousands of people danced in the streets.

_____ 2. The President _____ the terrorists for the bloody attack.

_____ 3. Sam's big eyes were _____ from his mother.

_____ 4. Finally, the _____ decided that the accused was innocent.

_____ 5. The cake got _____ because I sat on it accidentally.

III. 選擇題 (20%)

_____ 1. Troops and weapons were _____ outside the city.

(A) deployed   (B) thrilled   (C) presumed   (D) inherited

_____ 2. I'm designing a _____ that can detect radiation.

(A) sensor   (B) counselor   (C) viewpoint   (D) columnist

_____ 3. You must give _____ arguments to persuade your audience.

(A) perspective   (B) squashed   (C) minimized   (D) rational

_____ 4. Mr. Nguyen speaks Vietnamese with _____.

(A) carnival   (B) ballot   (C) fluency   (D) inheritance

_____ 5. Sarah was chosen to be the _____ to the current general manager.

(A) rhetoric   (B) successor   (C) jury   (D) undergraduate

Level 5-2 Test 9

Class: _____ No.: _____ Name: _____ Score: _____

I. 文意字彙 (40%)

_____ 1. Black is still the p_____g color of formal evening wear.

_____ 2. The speaker r_____ed on without noticing that most of the listeners had fallen asleep.

_____ 3. I have a c_____n to make—I spilled your perfume when you were out.

_____ 4. "U_____e the idiom, everybody. It is important," said the teacher.

_____ 5. Even a casual o_____r can tell the dramatic improvement of the polluted river.

II. 字彙配合 (請忽略大小寫) (40%)

(A) erupted	(B) vomited	(C) combat	(D) landlord	(E) banner

_____ 1. The workers demonstrated under the _____ of equal employment opportunities.

_____ 2. Since over 10,000 soldiers had died in _____, the general decided to retreat.

_____ 3. The _____ decided to lower our rent because we took good care of the apartment.

_____ 4. The boy was sick and _____ all he had eaten.

_____ 5. The situation turned chaotic after the fight _____ between the two rival gangs.

III. 選擇題 (20%)

_____ 1. Macau is known for many _____.

(A) forums (B) casinos (C) pessimists (D) banners

_____ 2. Is this issue outside or within the _____ of chemistry?

(A) combat (B) suite (C) optimism (D) domain

_____ 3. This movie is regarded as the best _____ ever made.

(A) thriller (B) missionary (C) landlord (D) credibility

_____ 4. The temperature _____ to 51°C, and many elders died from the heat.

(A) ribbed (B) vomited (C) soared (D) squatted

_____ 5. For _____ reasons, the businessman came back to his hometown.

(A) current (B) initiative (C) sentimental (D) depressing

Level 5-2 Test 10

Class: _____ No.: _____ Name: _____ Score: _____

I. 文意字彙 (40%)

_____ 1. The travel agent gave us a b_____h of travel brochures.

_____ 2. Father has his problems to worry about, so don't bother him with such p_____y matters.

_____ 3. I took the e_____r instead of the elevator to the third floor of the store.

_____ 4. The man was c_____ed to a wheelchair after the car crash.

_____ 5. The lifeguards are s_____sing the children swimming in the pool.

II. 字彙配合 (請忽略大小寫) (40%)

(A) creek	(B) ridge	(C) deputy	(D) moaned	(E) injected

_____ 1. The _____ used to be so clear that we could see fish in it.

_____ 2. The boy _____ when he was told to turn off the TV and go to bed.

_____ 3. Pigeons are resting on the _____ of the roof.

_____ 4. George is the _____ while his boss is on a business trip.

_____ 5. The nurse _____ people with COVID-19 vaccines.

III. 選擇題 (20%)

_____ 1. The hunter _____ the rabbit and then cooked it for lunch.

    (A) injected   (B) proclaimed   (C) undertook   (D) gutted

_____ 2. This _____ is valid till August and entitles you to 10% off all products.

    (A) intestine   (B) deputy   (C) voucher   (D) cemetery

_____ 3. The _____ of the exhibition hall was painted gold.

    (A) comedian   (B) laser   (C) creek   (D) dome

_____ 4. The scandal occurred when the old king was still on the _____.

    (A) throne   (B) instability   (C) realism   (D) moan

_____ 5. David asked his mother for forgiveness with _____.

    (A) odds   (B) sobs   (C) waiters   (D) servers

Level 5-2 Test 11

Class: _____ No.: _____ Name: _____ Score: _____

I. 文意字彙 (40%)

_____ 1. A l____r is responsible for making laws.

_____ 2. Judging from the woman's last name, we can tell she is
d____ded from a royal family.

_____ 3. Jimmy attended the summer s____n of the university.

_____ 4. The singer was c____ted with a bunch of questions on her age
when meeting the press.

_____ 5. My parents have been very busy and always have s____ks of
work to do.

II. 字彙配合 (請忽略大小寫) (40%)

(A) operational	(B) mode	(C) profound	(D) rifle	(E) vow

_____ 1. You can play the video game in easy, normal or hard _____.

_____ 2. The hunter went hunting in the woods with a(n) _____.

_____ 3. Edith made a(n) _____ that someday she would start her own business.

_____ 4. Some _____ problems in the new computer system caused the factory to
close up for a week.

_____ 5. The emotional trauma of Joe's childhood has a(n) _____ effect on his
personality.

III. 選擇題 (20%)

_____ 1. A mysterious stranger _____ a knife into the mayor's heart.

(A) betrayed (B) thrust (C) undid (D) hauled

_____ 2. Elizabeth was given a(n) _____ for diabetes.

(A) phase (B) mode (C) injection (D) estate

_____ 3. The old lady is _____ with severe knee pain.

(A) softened (B) vowed (C) crippled (D) donated

_____ 4. The author's book opened a new _____ of artificial intelligence.

(A) rifle (B) realm (C) commentary (D) ancestor

_____ 5. We are unable to predict whom Sharon will marry with any _____.

(A) certainty (B) legislator (C) fraction (D) betrayal

Level 5-2 Test 12

Class: _____ No.: _____ Name: _____ Score: _____

I. 文意字彙 (40%)

_____ 1. The factory is going to shut down. More than 1,000 workers face u_____t.

_____ 2. Much to my d_____r, the doctor confirmed that I had cancer.

_____ 3. The government officials didn't reach a c_____s on building the power plant.

_____ 4. The merchant stores the products in the w_____e before distributing them to retail stores.

_____ 5. It was found that the two policemen had been in l_____e with the drug dealer for many years.

II. 字彙配合 (請忽略大小寫) (40%)

(A) ethics	(B) hazards	(C) prohibited	(D) ticked	(E) stains

_____ 1. Cheating customers is a violation of business _____.

_____ 2. Pollution is one of the major _____ to wildlife.

_____ 3. To protect wild animals, hunting is strictly _____ in this mountainous area.

_____ 4. My mom can't get these coffee _____ out of the carpet.

_____ 5. I didn't sleep well because the clock _____ too noisily.

III. 選擇題 (20%)

_____ 1. Lisa's dream is to be a news _____.
(A) stain　　(B) donor　　(C) inning　　(D) commentator

_____ 2. As a _____ of this company, Ben will attend the annual conference this Tuesday.
(A) chapel　　(B) shareholder　　(C) fragment　　(D) rim

_____ 3. _____ images can be stored on a smartphone or computer.
(A) Molecular　　(B) Sole　　(C) Surplus　　(D) Photographic

_____ 4. After the successful operation, I felt _____ about my grandfather's health.
(A) reassured　　(B) prohibited　　(C) biased　　(D) prejudiced

_____ 5. A(n) _____ tends to look at things in a positive way.
(A) pessimist　　(B) optimist　　(C) criterion　　(D) tick

Level 5-2 Test 13

Class: _____ No.: _____ Name: _____ Score: _____

I. 文意字彙 (40%)

_____ 1. Our lives will be at s____e if the war breaks out.

_____ 2. This is only a c____e experiment, so the result may not be accurate.

_____ 3. My uncle has an o____d where he grows oranges and bananas.

_____ 4. Citizens over 20 have the c____l right to vote.

_____ 5. Don't just stand in the d____y. Come and help me carry the tools to the front yard.

II. 字彙配合 (請忽略大小寫) (40%)

(A) projection	(B) shattered	(C) suspended	(D) unfolded	(E) innovation

_____ 1. The explosion _____ all the windows of the houses near the area.

_____ 2. The man's driver's license was _____ for a year.

_____ 3. The sofa can be _____ to make a bed.

_____ 4. The _____ on the screen showed a skeleton of a prehistoric human.

_____ 5. The cellphone is a great _____ in the communication industry.

III. 選擇題 (20%)

_____ 1. The play is _____ as a tragedy.

(A) suspended　(B) ripped　(C) characterized　(D) tiled

_____ 2. We set up the _____ of the plan before we began.

(A) rebellion　(B) framework　(C) innovation　(D) morality

_____ 3. Although the _____ is second-hand, it is well maintained and still in good condition.

(A) pickup　(B) heir　(C) destiny　(D) solo

_____ 4. It takes much training and experience to be a good _____.

(A) inheritance　(B) legacy　(C) warrior　(D) projection

_____ 5. It is not _____ for a lawyer to reveal the client's confidences.

(A) bizarre　(B) rebellious　(C) ethical　(D) shattering

Level 5-2 Test 14

Class: _____ No.: _____ Name: _____ Score: _____

I. 文意字彙 (40%)

_____ 1. Ann bought the bananas from a fruit s____l in the market.

_____ 2. The man was sent to prison because he had committed the election f____d.

_____ 3. Gabriel didn't buy pizza d____h; he made it by himself.

_____ 4. An arrogant person is p____e to believe that he is superior to anyone else.

_____ 5. The politician's argument for economic growth struck a c____d with many people in the country.

II. 字彙配合 (請忽略大小寫) (40%)

(A) wary	(B) compact	(C) unlocked	(D) diagnosed	(E) exclaimed

_____ 1. Hank _____ that this was the most marvelous performance he'd ever seen.

_____ 2. Charlotte _____ the door of her car to let me get in.

_____ 3. Children should be taught to be _____ of strangers.

_____ 4. Brady would like to rent a(n) _____ car instead of a luxurious one.

_____ 5. Ellen was _____ as having heart disease.

III. 選擇題 (20%)

_____ 1. Cancer _____ in this area has been increasing.

    (A) constraint   (B) originality   (C) crystal   (D) mortality

_____ 2. Solar energy is a type of _____ energy, which can be used continuously without causing pollution.

    (A) legislative   (B) sustainable   (C) sheer   (D) herbal

_____ 3. Ted felt so sleepy that his vision _____.

    (A) exclaimed   (B) compacted   (C) blurred   (D) unlocked

_____ 4. The name of the _____ should be written in the middle of the envelope.

    (A) recipient   (B) rod   (C) inquiry   (D) investigation

_____ 5. As the typhoon came, huge waves swept over the _____ and struck the ships docked there.

    (A) restriction   (B) pier   (C) sophomore   (D) tin

進階英文字彙力 4501～6000PLUS 習題本

Level 5-2 Test 15

Class: _____ No.: _____ Name: _____ Score: _____

I. 文意字彙 (40%)

_____ 1. The ship f_____ted with lumber was bound for Kaohsiung.

_____ 2. Drinking alcohol could make you do many w_____d things that you normally wouldn't do.

_____ 3. It is the responsibility of the personnel department to r_____t new employees.

_____ 4. Computer technology is u_____ed every year. It's always improving.

_____ 5. The girl b_____hed when she noticed the handsome boy was looking at her.

II. 字彙配合 (請忽略大小寫) (40%)

(A) propaganda	(B) hockey	(C) outfits	(D) chores	(E) torch

_____ 1. Kimberly is always dressed in smart business _____ when she goes to work.

_____ 2. My job is to do the administrative _____ of the office.

_____ 3. Bruno and I held a(n) _____ while going through the dark tunnel.

_____ 4. The girls play _____ on ice in winter.

_____ 5. The mass media should not make _____ for any specific political party.

III. 選擇題 (20%)

_____ 1. The Koran is _____ to all Muslims.

    (A) insane   (B) compassionate (C) sacred   (D) strange

_____ 2. The man has _____ of over ten million dollars.

    (A) pillars   (B) chores   (C) dialects   (D) liabilities

_____ 3. The lawyer charges a low fee for _____.

    (A) hockey   (B) sovereignty (C) custody   (D) consultation

_____ 4. Alice _____ her apple for her brother's orange.

    (A) swapped   (B) excluded   (C) outfitted   (D) mortgaged

_____ 5. The local _____ has already arrested the robbers.

    (A) torch   (B) sheriff   (C) driveway   (D) stance

Level 5-2 Test 16

Class: _____ No.: _____ Name: _____ Score: _____

I. 文意字彙 (40%)

_____ 1. When the fire alarm went off, all the audience b_____ted for the exit.

_____ 2. It is not healthy to suppress one's feelings. Everyone should find a proper o____t for his or her emotions.

_____ 3. Chest pain can be one of the s____ms of a heart attack.

_____ 4. Because of the thunder, Alex's dog kept w____ning outside last night.

_____ 5. The trunk of the tree is about ten foot in d____r.

II. 字彙配合 (請忽略大小寫) (40%)

(A) lounge	(B) frontier	(C) exclusive	(D) ego	(E) honorable

_____ 1. I praised the kid for his performance on stage to boost his _____.

_____ 2. The swimming pool is _____ to the members of the club.

_____ 3. We agreed to meet at the student _____ after school.

_____ 4. Many people think teaching was a(n) _____ profession.

_____ 5. A(n) _____ is a border between two countries.

III. 選擇題 (20%)

_____ 1. Surprisingly, it took me only a short time to go through _____ at the airport.
  (A) prophets   (B) customs   (C) regimes   (D) egos

_____ 2. Professor Wang is _____ with too many administrative jobs.
  (A) compelled   (B) startled   (C) gobbled   (D) saddled

_____ 3. My father-in-law has suffered from a(n) _____ kidney disease for years.
  (A) exclusive   (B) chronic   (C) spacious   (D) honorable

_____ 4. The rent does not include _____ such as water and electricity.
  (A) utilities   (B) frontiers   (C) motives   (D) indications

_____ 5. The government plans to build gas _____ here for strategic reasons.
  (A) shields   (B) lounges   (C) pipelines   (D) tournaments

16

Level 5-2 Test 17

Class: _____ No.: _____ Name: _____ Score: _____

I. 文意字彙 (40%)

_____ 1. With his mouth full, the boy m_____ed something that I couldn't hear clearly.

_____ 2. The kid s_____red at the thought of staying in such a dark room alone.

_____ 3. I tried in vain to i_____e myself into the new community.

_____ 4. The pretty lake was s_____ling in the sunlight.

_____ 5. It is said that the p_____es would attack the ships at sea and take away valuables.

II. 字彙配合 (請忽略大小寫) (40%)

(A) tackle	(B) traitor	(C) utilize	(D) compensation	(E) wig

_____ 1. That man is a(n) _____ who sells secrets to the enemy.

_____ 2. People have learned to _____ solar power as a source of energy.

_____ 3. Mary wore a blonde _____ and dark glasses, trying to disguise herself.

_____ 4. The government carried out economic policies to _____ inflation.

_____ 5. The airline paid the passenger US$500 in _____ for her lost luggage.

III. 選擇題 (20%)

_____ 1. Eco-friendly parents tend not to use disposable _____ on their babies.

    (A) diapers   (B) wigs   (C) chunks   (D) debuts

_____ 2. The _____ of the new policy went well.

    (A) tackle   (B) execution   (C) compensation   (D) reinforcement

_____ 3. When kids are growing up, the sex _____ in their bodies increase.

    (A) bonuses   (B) galaxies   (C) hormones   (D) traitors

_____ 4. The fisherman _____ his fishing boat out of the harbor.

    (A) steered   (B) lumped   (C) utilized   (D) proportioned

_____ 5. Even though I have been living in London for 15 years, I still feel like a(n) _____ here.

    (A) emission   (B) salmon   (C) ratio   (D) outsider

Level 5-2 Test 18

Class: _____ No.: _____ Name: _____ Score: _____

I. 文意字彙 (40%)

_____ 1. Vegetables and fruit are good for your d____n.

_____ 2. That part of the country is just a w____s. No one lives there.

_____ 3. The old temple has fallen into d____y because of lack of care.

_____ 4. Our company tried to reduce the o____d to stay in business.

_____ 5. John spent a night in the t____t lounge at Gatwick Airport.

II. 字彙配合 (請忽略大小寫) (40%)

(A) tangle	(B) variable	(C) municipal	(D) hostage	(E) exile

_____ 1. The politician criticized the government and was sent into _____.

_____ 2. My younger brother is studying in that _____ library.

_____ 3. People on that train were taken _____ by several terrorists.

_____ 4. The quality of this restaurant is _____. Sometimes you can enjoy a tasty meal, but sometimes the food is terrible.

_____ 5. I usually wake up in the morning with my hair in a(n) _____.

III. 選擇題 (20%)

_____ 1. The poem _____ in my report was written by T. S. Eliot.

(A) stereotyped　　(B) tangled　　(C) cited　　(D) shoved

_____ 2. The _____ promised to repair the elevators within a day.

(A) variable　　(B) booth　　(C) contractor　　(D) placement

_____ 3. The old man was rushed to the hospital for a(n) _____ after he fell down.

(A) gasp　　(B) mandate　　(C) exile　　(D) scan

_____ 4. The politician's supporters totally _____ what he said in the speech.

(A) specialized　　(B) endorsed　　(C) rendered　　(D) skimmed

_____ 5. The detective sat in the back _____, observing the man at the bar.

(A) booth　　(B) prosecution　　(C) hostage　　(D) integration

Level 5-2 Test 19

Class: _____ No.: _____ Name: _____ Score: _____

I. 文意字彙 (40%)

_____ 1. The boss e_____ts those workers who are young and naive.

_____ 2. Sam measured the d_____ns of the room before buying some new furniture.

_____ 3. The will s_____fied exactly who should receive the old man's fortune.

_____ 4. Greed t_____ted the judge to take bribes.

_____ 5. When the politician was asked about the bribery scandal, he just s_____ged his shoulders and said nothing.

II. 字彙配合 (請忽略大小寫) (40%)

(A) masculine	(B) scar	(C) overwhelming	(D) boredom	(E) plural

_____ 1. The car accident left a(n) _____ on her right arm.

_____ 2. Deep voice and facial hair are _____ characteristics.

_____ 3. Mice is the _____ form of mouse.

_____ 4. Ann was homesick. She had a(n) _____ desire to return home.

_____ 5. Rita paced the floor out of sheer _____.

III. 選擇題 (20%)

_____ 1. The ambitious young man has started a new _____ of his own.

    (A) boredom   (B) generator   (C) unity   (D) enterprise

_____ 2. The dishonest salesperson _____ the lady into signing an unfair contract.

    (A) deceived   (B) stewed   (C) overwhelmed   (D) scarred

_____ 3. Rebecca is applying for German _____.

    (A) integrity   (B) measurement   (C) citizenship   (D) mustard

_____ 4. Quebec is the largest _____ in Canada.

    (A) vein   (B) province   (C) hostility   (D) contradiction

_____ 5. Yesterday morning, Sam found that the _____ of his car had been covered with snow.

    (A) compliance   (B) transition   (C) windshield   (D) rental

Level 5-2 Test 20

Class: _____ No.: _____ Name: _____ Score: _____

I. 文意字彙 (40%)

_____ 1. Emma has been e_____c about classical music since she was ten years old.

_____ 2. The delay of our flight added another c_____n to our trip.

_____ 3. Dragons are m_____l creatures. I don't believe they really exist.

_____ 4. The candidate said he would d_____e himself to children's welfare.

_____ 5. Rather than drive my car, I like to take the s_____e bus to the office.

II. 字彙配合 (請忽略大小寫) (40%)

(A) myth	(B) massage	(C) treaty	(D) boundary	(E) quiver

_____ 1. These high mountains mark the _____ between the two nations.

_____ 2. The story about mermaids is a _____.

_____ 3. A good _____ helps relieve both physical and emotional stress.

_____ 4. Mary felt a _____ of fear when the stranger approached her.

_____ 5. The president signed a peace _____ with that country.

III. 選擇題 (20%)

_____ 1. The radical tax reform has caused much _____.

    (A) massage   (B) controversy   (C) exploration   (D) repayment

_____ 2. I clicked on the _____ to start the app, but nothing happened.

    (A) yacht   (B) icon   (C) treaty   (D) particle

_____ 3. The wolf's howl _____ the little kids.

    (A) intensified   (B) poked   (C) heightened   (D) terrified

_____ 4. It was _____ to learn the piano when I was a kid.

    (A) worthwhile   (B) tactful   (C) civic   (D) diplomatic

_____ 5. More than 20,000 _____ were watching the live performance.

    (A) venues   (B) scenarios   (C) spectators   (D) boundaries

Level 6 Test 1

Class: _____ No.: _____ Name: _____ Score: _____

I. 文意字彙 (40%)

_____ 1. To speak English well, you should learn to pronounce both vowels and c_____ts correctly.

_____ 2. Mrs. Simpson's c_____l necklace goes perfectly with her pink dress.

_____ 3. To our a_____e, the couple sitting in front of us kept talking loudly in the concert.

_____ 4. You can d_____h the hood from your coat if you don't need it.

_____ 5. The store sells a variety of m_____e. You can get almost everything you want there.

II. 字彙配合 (請忽略大小寫) (40%)

(A) veil	(B) notorious	(C) hospitable	(D) courtyard	(E) broth

_____ 1. The soup made with _____ is more delicious than that with water.

_____ 2. The lady is very _____ to anyone who visits her.

_____ 3. A _____ is partly or completely enclosed by the walls of a building.

_____ 4. The city is _____ for its crimes and drugs.

_____ 5. The groom lifted the bride's _____ and kissed her.

III. 選擇題 (20%)

_____ 1. If my _____ is correct, you have been reading this book for 40 minutes.

(A) crossing (B) nickel (C) courtyard (D) arithmetic

_____ 2. Some _____ expressions are not suitable for formal occasions.

(A) hospitable (B) bilateral (C) colloquial (D) welcoming

_____ 3. _____ pudding is my favorite dessert.

(A) Broth (B) Vanilla (C) Admiral (D) Eternity

_____ 4. The political prisoner was _____ from the labor camp.

(A) enriched (B) strangled (C) veiled (D) liberated

_____ 5. Supporters will hold a rally to show their _____ tomorrow.

(A) solidarity (B) radius (C) product (D) trek

Level 6 Test 2

Class: _____ No.: _____ Name: _____ Score: _____

I. 文意字彙 (40%)

_____ 1. Sandra is taking a _____cs for her infected wound in the leg.

_____ 2. The medication can s_____e your sore throat.

_____ 3. Bill walked on c_____hes after the car accident.

_____ 4. The girl found a flock of ducks swimming u_____h the bridge.

_____ 5. My mother's eyes b_____ed with fury when she learned that I had cheated on the exam.

II. 字彙配合 (請忽略大小寫) (40%)

(A) examiner	(B) comet	(C) cement	(D) versatile	(E) cumulative

_____ 1. Halley's _____ can be seen from the earth about every 76 years.

_____ 2. Tom's _____ teaching experience finally made him a distinguished teacher.

_____ 3. Emily is a(n) _____ actress. She is good at acting, singing, and writing plays.

_____ 4. _____ can be used to build houses.

_____ 5. The student became very nervous because the _____ looked serious.

III. 選擇題 (20%)

_____ 1. The farmer _____ over a ditch, chasing the runaway pig.

   (A) strode   (B) mimicked   (C) oriented   (D) ascended

_____ 2. The engineer checked the system for _____.

   (A) conspiracies   (B) examiners   (C) plots   (D) defects

_____ 3. This monument is a symbol of _____ between the two countries.

   (A) cement   (B) nourishment   (C) brotherhood   (D) rap

_____ 4. There will be thousands of _____ taking the listening test at school tomorrow.

   (A) mixtures   (B) examinees   (C) imitators   (D) comets

_____ 5. Bill is an experienced lawyer and acts in a(n) _____ role in our company.

   (A) cumulative   (B) hybrid   (C) advisory   (D) nourishing

Level 6 Test 3

Class: _____ No.: _____ Name: _____ Score: _____

I. 文意字彙 (40%)

_____ 1. Rita's memory of the tragic accident has l_____red on for over ten years.

_____ 2. To prevent the infectious disease from spreading, everyone should be aware of personal h_____e.

_____ 3. Losing both of her parents, the little girl was raised in an o_____e.

_____ 4. *The Boy Who Cried Wolf* is a famous f_____e that tells readers the importance of being honest.

_____ 5. The police caught the v_____n who set fire to the gas station.

II. 字彙配合 (請忽略大小寫) (40%)

(A) applicable	(B) sorrowful	(C) bleach	(D) excerpt	(E) oath

_____ 1. Without using _____, it's impossible to get rid of the stain.

_____ 2. Remember you are now under _____. All you say must be the truth.

_____ 3. No rule is _____ to every situation. There is always an exception.

_____ 4. A(n) _____ from Joanne's speech will appear in today's newspapers.

_____ 5. What a(n) _____ sight it is to see a starving child begging on the street!

III. 選擇題 (20%)

_____ 1. Most of our preferences are _____.

    (A) sorrowful   (B) subjective   (C) sad   (D) energetic

_____ 2. Differences of opinion among the colleagues may lead to _____.

    (A) realization   (B) contention   (C) detention   (D) bleach

_____ 3. The mayor took _____ measures to fight against crime.

    (A) drastic   (B) objective   (C) cynical   (D) vigorous

_____ 4. It is important to have a(n) _____ on a regular basis.

    (A) affiliate   (B) oath   (C) census   (D) commonwealth

_____ 5. The mother bear would do anything to protect her _____.

    (A) excerpts   (B) glaciers   (C) bureaucrats   (D) cubs

Level 6

Level 6 Test 4

Class: _____ No.: _____ Name: _____ Score: _____

I. 文意字彙 (40%)

_____ 1. The f____e of roses fills the beautiful garden.

_____ 2. A l____d is a type of reptile with four legs and a long tail.

_____ 3. My friend goes jogging every day to burn off e____s fat.

_____ 4. Some students took those easy courses just to a____e credits.

_____ 5. The politician was a____ted, and the police still didn't know who killed him.

II. 字彙配合 (請忽略大小寫) (40%)

| (A) outward | (B) offspring | (C) odor | (D) vitality | (E) reckless |

_____ 1. My brother took a shower to get rid of his terrible body _____.

_____ 2. It was _____ of Dan to go mountain-climbing without checking the weather report first.

_____ 3. The eighty-year-old man is still full of _____. He participates in lots of activities.

_____ 4. Mr. Smith's property was divided among his _____.

_____ 5. Never judge people purely by _____ appearances.

III. 選擇題 (20%)

_____ 1. Social workers are normally patient and _____.

    (A) reckless   (B) imperial   (C) rash   (D) communicative

_____ 2. Julia's _____ to her studies impressed her professor.

    (A) cucumber   (B) offspring   (C) dedication   (D) spaceship

_____ 3. _____ have been used by human beings since the dawn of recorded history.

    (A) Outbreaks   (B) Ceramics   (C) Contestants   (D) Astronauts

_____ 4. To avoid traffic jams, we _____ the busy city center and took another route.

    (A) illuminated   (B) confirmed   (C) bypassed   (D) deterred

_____ 5. An unmanned _____ has successfully returned to Earth.

    (A) spacecraft   (B) vigor   (C) surname   (D) odor

Level 6 Test 5

Class: _____ No.: _____ Name: _____ Score: _____

I. 文意字彙 (40%)

_____ 1. The ugly chimney was a b_____t on the landscape here.

_____ 2. My sister has worked as an a_____e at a beauty salon for about three years to learn the craft of hairdressing.

_____ 3. It is a difficult task to c_____e such a comprehensive dictionary.

_____ 4. It is cruel of you to say o_____t that you don't love Mia anymore.

_____ 5. Mrs. Mitchell bought an o_____l carpet as a souvenir of her trip to India.

II. 字彙配合 (請忽略大小寫) (40%)

(A) wardrobe　　(B) longevity　　(C) recreational　　(D) spontaneous　　(E) aboriginal

_____ 1. Irene's speech was so _____ that words seemed to be flowing out of her mouth and touching the hearts of the audience.

_____ 2. Some government officials suggested that the land should be returned to the _____ people.

_____ 3. We wished Ken health and _____ on his birthday.

_____ 4. Hiking is a very good _____ activity.

_____ 5. The little boy hid himself in the _____ while playing hide-and-seek with the other kids.

III. 選擇題 (20%)

_____ 1. Several episodes in the film lack _____.

　　(A) continuity　　(B) indifference　　(C) asthma　　(D) longevity

_____ 2. Chester tried to _____ an image as a reliable leader.

　　(A) symbolize　　(B) cultivate　　(C) outnumber　　(D) certify

_____ 3. Sarah spent all her time with her boyfriend to the _____ of her other friends.

　　(A) wardrobe　　(B) literacy　　(C) exclusion　　(D) airway

_____ 4. The museum _____ told me not to take pictures in the building.

　　(A) attendant　　(B) calculator　　(C) aboriginal　　(D) detergent

_____ 5. The firefighters made _____ attempts to control the fire.

　　(A) spontaneous　　(B) frantic　　(C) dental　　(D) recreational

Level 6

Level 6 Test 6

Class: _____ No.: _____ Name: _____ Score: _____

I. 文意字彙 (40%)

_____ 1. If you r_____e the speech beforehand, you will not be so nervous when you are giving it.

_____ 2. What if an unstoppable spear meets an immovable shield? It is a well-known p_____x.

_____ 3. Ella is d_____red by anxiety because her son is missing.

_____ 4. The minister has been in the s_____t since the revelation of his sex scandal.

_____ 5. The father is rocking the cradle gently and singing a l_____y to comfort his baby.

II. 字彙配合 (請忽略大小寫) (40%)

(A) champagne	(B) algebra	(C) weary	(D) solitary	(E) calligraphy

_____ 1. _____ is a type of mathematics in which signs and letters are used to represent numbers.

_____ 2. The studying center is almost empty except for a(n) _____ figure.

_____ 3. Let's pop a bottle of _____ to celebrate our victory!

_____ 4. _____ is beautiful and artistic handwriting created with a special brush.

_____ 5. After finishing the marathon, all the runners look _____ but satisfied.

III. 選擇題 (20%)

_____ 1. The scarf _____ your coat perfectly.

    (A) gobbles   (B) grazes   (C) induces   (D) complements

_____ 2. This style of dancing was _____ in Argentine.

    (A) contradicted   (B) highlighted   (C) wearied   (D) originated

_____ 3. The knife is a little bit _____ and needs sharpening.

    (A) lunar   (B) astray   (C) blunt   (D) solitary

_____ 4. If you cannot put a(n) _____ on spending, you will go bankrupt one day.

    (A) fascination   (B) curb   (C) oyster   (D) banquet

_____ 5. The cargo ship is _____ for Singapore.

    (A) sharp   (B) awesome   (C) destined   (D) complementary

Level 6 Test 7

Class: _____ No.: _____ Name: _____ Score: _____

I. 文意字彙 (40%)

_____ 1. Anna's rosy c_____n indicates her good health.

_____ 2. It's hard for me to d_____e between male and female birds. They look very much alike.

_____ 3. Kevin's room was o_____ted with beautiful photos.

_____ 4. A b_____r of Arts degree takes three to four years of full-time study in Taiwan.

_____ 5. The woman has difficulty getting pregnant because of some f_____y problems.

II. 字彙配合 (請忽略大小寫) (40%)

(A) peacock	(B) woodpecker	(C) captive	(D) anthem	(E) lush

_____ 1. A(n) _____ is a big bird; the male can spread out its tail feathers to show off the bright colors.

_____ 2. A(n) _____ uses its beak to make holes in tree trunks.

_____ 3. Before the match, they played the national _____ of the host country.

_____ 4. Sue stood by the window, looking at the _____ garden where hundreds of flowers were in full bloom.

_____ 5. Hundreds of people in the theater were held _____ by some terrorists.

III. 選擇題 (20%)

_____ 1. The boat had to sail around the _____ before it could enter the harbor.

    (A) cape   (B) anthem   (C) curfew   (D) stimulation

_____ 2. Sue _____ from Robert's statement that he supported gender equality.

    (A) convened   (B) alienated   (C) inferred   (D) dictated

_____ 3. The _____ discovered a planet that was likely to have water.

    (A) chemists   (B) astronomers   (C) pianists   (D) woodpeckers

_____ 4. Mr. Watson's only _____ is chewing betel nuts.

    (A) peacock   (B) vice   (C) grease   (D) infertility

_____ 5. The virus spreads through contact with blood, semen, and other _____ fluids.

    (A) relentless   (B) outgoing   (C) lush   (D) bodily

Level 6

Level 6 Test 8

Class: _____ No.: _____ Name: _____ Score: _____

I. 文意字彙 (40%)

_____ 1. During the rainy season, the river usually o_____ws and floods the fields along the river bank.

_____ 2. Sam only uses organic f_____r to enrich the soil of his farm.

_____ 3. Nora used a lot of makeup to cover the p_____es on her face.

_____ 4. The secretary took d_____n from the manager and sent his messages to other departments.

_____ 5. Do you know how to c_____e the distance between the earth and the moon?

II. 字彙配合 (請忽略大小寫) (40%)

(A) harness	(B) disastrous	(C) maiden	(D) bosom	(E) capsule

_____ 1. Cathy put a _____ on the horse and rode away.

_____ 2. If you don't read the safety instructions carefully, you may suffer _____ consequences.

_____ 3. The sinking of the Titanic on her _____ voyage was made into a movie.

_____ 4. The baby fell asleep in her mother's warm _____.

_____ 5. Medicine is usually in the form of a pill, a tablet or a _____.

III. 選擇題 (20%)

_____ 1. Two-thirds of the _____ is affected by the new labor policy.

    (A) curry   (B) suspension   (C) workforce   (D) attainment

_____ 2. The police found the little boy's _____ in a cave and assumed that he had been murdered.

    (A) capsule   (B) abundance   (C) subscription   (D) corpse

_____ 3. The _____ rain has caused floods in many places.

    (A) persistent   (B) maiden   (C) chestnut   (D) eccentric

_____ 4. Mom carefully _____ the flowerpots on the windowsill.

    (A) achieved   (B) inflicted   (C) aligned   (D) calculated

_____ 5. The school _____ patrols the campus every night.

    (A) harness   (B) caretaker   (C) remainder   (D) bosom

Level 6 Test 9

Class: _____ No.: _____ Name: _____ Score: _____

I. 文意字彙 (40%)

_____ 1. The milk is f_____fied with vitamin E and calcium.

_____ 2. The p_____r bears are endangered largely as a result of global warming.

_____ 3. Harper didn't become a p_____t until she became aware of her country's difficult situation.

_____ 4. A d_____r rules a country with absolute power.

_____ 5. Some workers were made redundant and laid off because of the c_____n of the factory.

II. 字彙配合 (請忽略大小寫) (40%)

| (A) preventive | (B) reproductions | (C) captions | (D) synonyms | (E) majestic |

_____ 1. Jimmy decorates his new house with _____ of famous paintings.

_____ 2. People must take _____ measures against the coming typhoon.

_____ 3. "Small" and "little" are _____.

_____ 4. Read the _____ under the picture and you'll know what it is about.

_____ 5. In the distance stand the _____ Alps, with snow-capped peaks shining in the sun.

III. 選擇題 (20%)

_____ 1. Our company's annual _____ will take place next Monday.

    (A) booklet   (B) audit   (C) abbreviation   (D) synonym

_____ 2. The tribes _____ the rainforest all the year round.

    (A) allege   (B) caption   (C) inhabit   (D) abbreviate

_____ 3. Some Thai dishes are very spicy, as they contain a lot of _____ and other spices.

    (A) chilies   (B) boulevards   (C) chants   (D) haunts

_____ 4. This best-selling _____ cream uses traditional herbal ingredients.

    (A) majestic   (B) usual   (C) cosmetic   (D) customary

_____ 5. Practicing _____ helps me sleep better.

    (A) discharge   (B) reproduction   (C) acclaim   (D) yoga

Level 6

Level 6 Test 10

Class: _____ No.: _____ Name: _____ Score: _____

I. 文意字彙 (40%)

_____ 1. Lisa often cooks h_____l food for her children, like chicken soup and brown rice.

_____ 2. The sunflower oil contains less c_____l and is better for our health.

_____ 3. Many animals do not breed well in c_____y after they are taken away from their natural habitat.

_____ 4. This country was once a military d_____p.

_____ 5. These workers are d_____e. We decide to stop hiring them.

II. 字彙配合 (請忽略大小寫) (40%)

(A) inquired	(B) cigar	(C) auditorium	(D) anchor	(E) dazzled

_____ 1. John was _____ by the strong sunlight and could hardly see anything.

_____ 2. Uncle Jack called me and _____ about my father's condition.

_____ 3. Listen to the captain, and then you'll know the time to cast _____.

_____ 4. After dinner, my grandfather lit a(n) _____, blowing smoke into the air.

_____ 5. The _____ can hold 40,000 people.

III. 選擇題 (20%)

_____ 1. Participants must act in _____ with the rules.

(A) accordance (B) breadth (C) prose (D) boxing

_____ 2. Mary cannot _____ the idea of living with her mother-in-law.

(A) synthesize (B) dazzle (C) flake (D) abide

_____ 3. My sister uses _____ to make herself look more beautiful.

(A) pharmacies (B) flakes (C) auditoriums (D) cosmetics

_____ 4. The spectators _____ at the magician's skills.

(A) marveled (B) resided (C) anchored (D) inquired

_____ 5. The veteran managed to make contact with several _____ of his from wartime.

(A) cigars (B) comrades (C) alligators (D) prototypes

Level 6 Test 11

Class: _____ No.: _____ Name: _____ Score: _____

I. 文意字彙 (40%)

_____ 1. It is not p_____e to eat in the library.

_____ 2. The minister met with several European c_____ts to discuss how to stabilize the region's economy.

_____ 3. Politicians should be a_____e for the promises they make to the people.

_____ 4. The p_____t won the Academy Award for Best Original Screenplay.

_____ 5. F_____e is the traditional stories of a particular people or country.

II. 字彙配合 (請忽略大小寫) (40%)

(A) retrieve	(B) dispense	(C) mingle	(D) boycott	(E) tenant

_____ 1. The machine allows us to _____ with a lot of labor.

_____ 2. The _____ intentionally trashed the house for ridiculous reasons.

_____ 3. The software can help _____ deleted or lost files.

_____ 4. People called for a _____ against the shop for it sold expired food.

_____ 5. When you go to a party, you should try to be sociable and _____ with others.

III. 選擇題 (20%)

_____ 1. The government has made it clear that no _____ will be made to the demonstrators.

    (A) tenants   (B) imperatives   (C) concessions   (D) dramatists

_____ 2. Simon _____ his eyes from the broken limbs of his fellow soldiers.

    (A) radiated   (B) averted   (C) deafened   (D) mingled

_____ 3. This bookshelf was so _____ that we couldn't get it through the door.

    (A) civilized   (B) vital   (C) respective   (D) bulky

_____ 4. My dad made a dollhouse out of _____.

    (A) cardboard   (B) astronomy   (C) retrieval   (D) diesel

_____ 5. The brave dog secured the store against the _____.

    (A) boycott   (B) collision   (C) intruder   (D) aluminum

Level 6

Level 6 Test 12

Class: _____ No.: _____ Name: _____ Score: _____

I. 文意字彙 (40%)

_____ 1. The worker is tightening the screw with a s_____r.

_____ 2. Rachel prefers to go swimming to r_____h herself in summer.

_____ 3. Nancy felt uncomfortable a_____d so many people.

_____ 4. The price is 80 dollars i_____e of tax.

_____ 5. Rita spent a lot of time with her friend. Friendship is i_____e to her.

II. 字彙配合 (請忽略大小寫) (40%)

(A) coupons	(B) tentative	(C) robust	(D) concise	(E) abstractions

_____ 1. Sally saves all kinds of _____ so that she can buy things at lower prices.

_____ 2. John is almost 90 years old, but he remains _____.

_____ 3. Some people find philosophy hard to understand because they think it is full of _____.

_____ 4. The applicant gave the interviewer a(n) _____ smile and started to make her self-introduction.

_____ 5. Kevin's _____ explanation clarified all of our doubts.

III. 選擇題 (20%)

_____ 1. A study suggests that _____ has a significant effect on sleep disturbance.
(A) diplomacy (B) caffeine (C) aviation (D) pneumonia

_____ 2. Both reading and meeting different people _____ the mind.
(A) deduct (B) broaden (C) brace (D) diversify

_____ 3. The director spoke up for the _____ and lesbian community through her documentary.
(A) gay (B) resistant (C) miraculous (D) concise

_____ 4. The _____ of evidence gradually gave us a clear picture of the bribery case.
(A) accumulation (B) abstraction (C) coupon (D) brace

_____ 5. North, east, south, and west are the 4 _____ directions.
(A) robust (B) exclusive (C) comparative (D) cardinal

Level 6 Test 13

Class: _____ No.: _____ Name: _____ Score: _____

I. 文意字彙 (40%)

_____ 1. G_____y speaking, the equator is an imaginary line that divides the earth into the northern and southern hemispheres.

_____ 2. Studies show that a c_____e is intelligent and emotional enough to appreciate natural beauty.

_____ 3. The sales manager p_____red on the reasons why the new product couldn't bring in the profits as expected.

_____ 4. After Jimmy graduated from high school, he attended a military a_____y.

_____ 5. It is not easy to c_____e a 600-page novel into a 90-minute film.

II. 字彙配合 (請忽略大小寫) (40%)

(A) servings	(B) carefree	(C) renowned	(D) compasses	(E) virgin

_____ 1. Although I am over 60 years old, I still remember my _____ childhood.

_____ 2. It is awful that there are only few _____ forests left in the world.

_____ 3. Without a pair of _____, I can't draw a perfect circle.

_____ 4. How many _____ of vegetables do you eat every day?

_____ 5. Stephen King, a _____ writer of horror fiction, has published more than fifty books.

III. 選擇題 (20%)

_____ 1. The area has been _____ inhabitable by government officials.

    (A) compassed   (B) held   (C) deemed   (D) clasped

_____ 2. Students can learn more efficiently by applying a(n) _____ learning strategy.

    (A) analytical   (B) naughty   (C) virgin   (D) cowardly

_____ 3. Believe it or not, it _____ rains after I have my hair cut.

    (A) mischievously   (B) thereafter   (C) awhile   (D) invariably

_____ 4. Dr. Kim is a woman of great _____.

    (A) puberty   (B) intellect   (C) adolescence   (D) royalty

_____ 5. The department store sells different types of _____.

    (A) servings   (B) diversions   (C) brassieres   (D) directives

Level 6

Level 6 Test 14

Class: _____ No.: _____ Name: _____ Score: _____

I. 文意字彙 (40%)

_____ 1. D_____s is a disease in which someone has too much sugar in their blood.

_____ 2. G_____y is mathematics concerning the study and measurement of lines, angles, and shapes.

_____ 3. Penny doesn't have the b_____e to defend her ideas.

_____ 4. Ben and I saw the p_____ws of several upcoming films in the movie theater.

_____ 5. S_____n is the process of keeping places clean and hygienic.

II. 字彙配合 (請忽略大小寫) (40%)

(A) cashier	(B) downward	(C) irritated	(D) intimidated	(E) breakdown

_____ 1. The economy is on a(n) _____ trend. It goes from bad to worse.

_____ 2. Larry suffered from a nervous _____ because of his heavy workload.

_____ 3. Don't get _____ by the number of competitors.

_____ 4. Jane is not suitable for the job as a(n) _____ because she is poor at calculation.

_____ 5. The teacher got a bit _____ by his foolish questions.

III. 選擇題 (20%)

_____ 1. John's face was _____ with joy at the sight of his wife.
   (A) rallied　　　(B) animated　　　(C) disabled　　　(D) intimidated

_____ 2. Cindy's _____ with Bill lasted just a few weeks.
   (A) default　　　(B) correspondence (C) breakdown　　　(D) clearance

_____ 3. This artist's sculpture has many _____ values.
   (A) downward　　(B) disabled　　　(C) snug　　　(D) aesthetic

_____ 4. Patrick's mom is _____ about his chances of success.
   (A) cozy　　　(B) scenic　　　(C) skeptical　　　(D) catastrophic

_____ 5. The bride is wearing a white gown with matching _____.
   (A) accessories　　(B) spines　　　(C) confederations (D) cashiers

Level 6 Test 15

Class: _____ No.: _____ Name: _____ Score: _____

I. 文意字彙 (40%)

_____ 1. More and more parents show their d____f in the present educational reform.

_____ 2. Building a school in her hometown is Judy's l____g goal.

_____ 3. The famous s____r is thinking about the design of the statue.

_____ 4. It is a growing problem that more and more families collapse owing to the b____p of marriage.

_____ 5. Luckily, there were no c____ties in the bombing.

II. 字彙配合 (請忽略大小寫) (40%)

(A) affectionate   (B) congressman   (C) credible   (D) chairperson   (E) climax

_____ 1. The _____ of the film is a car chase on the highway.

_____ 2. If something is _____, it deserves to be trusted.

_____ 3. A(n) _____ is a member of the U.S. Congress.

_____ 4. Whenever I call on my grandmother, she greets me with a(n) _____ hug.

_____ 5. The _____, the head of the organization, decides who can speak in today's meeting.

III. 選擇題 (20%)

_____ 1. The _____ movie star attracted a lot of fans wherever he went.

　(A) credible　　(B) contemptuous　(C) believable　　(D) glamorous

_____ 2. Both the patient's upper and lower _____ were swollen, so it's hard for her to open her eyes.

　(A) congressmen　(B) chairs　　(C) eyelids　　(D) transcripts

_____ 3. The snobbish man _____ anyone whose salary is lower than his.

　(A) scorns　　(B) eclipses　　(C) sneezes　　(D) climaxes

_____ 4. The audience waited for the arrival of the rock star with eager _____.

　(A) anticipation　(B) defiance　　(C) modernization　(D) jade

_____ 5. The famous actress is under a false _____.

　(A) badge　　(B) accusation　　(C) addiction　　(D) crackdown

Level 6 Test 16

Class: _____ No.: _____ Name: _____ Score: _____

I. 文意字彙 (40%)

_____ 1. We have to hire more people to l_____n the increased workload.

_____ 2. Laziness is Jason's major f_____w.

_____ 3. The a_____m of "polite" is "rude."

_____ 4. Many people like the s_____y of the design. They don't like complicated things.

_____ 5. Running out of fuel, the truck began to lose m_____m.

II. 字彙配合 (請忽略大小寫) (40%)

(A) charitable	(B) jingle	(C) gleam	(D) conquest	(E) sociable

_____ 1. It looks like the World Cup will be the French team's next _____.

_____ 2. The orphanage is supported by _____ donations only.

_____ 3. Give it another try. There is still a _____ of hope.

_____ 4. Kids love to sing along with this advertising _____.

_____ 5. Serena was very _____. She enjoys meeting and talking to people.

III. 選擇題 (20%)

_____ 1. Andy lives in a small _____ in the center of the city.

　　(A) dwelling　　(B) defect　　(C) trillion　　(D) gleam

_____ 2. Tina is very _____ about whom she lets into her life.

　　(A) clockwise　　(B) selective　　(C) barbaric　　(D) sociable

_____ 3. People who _____ waste into the lake will be fined.

　　(A) discard　　(B) jingle　　(C) bribe　　(D) discomfort

_____ 4. Ryan likes to eat _____ with jam.

　　(A) opposites　　(B) caterers　　(C) probes　　(D) crackers

_____ 5. The manager offered a(n) _____ solution to customer complaints.

　　(A) accustomed　　(B) unsociable　　(C) definitive　　(D) indecisive

Level 6 Test 17

Class: _____ No.: _____ Name: _____ Score: _____

I. 文意字彙 (40%)

_____ 1. People often buy new winter g_____ts for Chinese New Year.

_____ 2. They took d_____y action against several soldiers who violated the rule.

_____ 3. Three meetings were c_____med into Sophia's busy schedule.

_____ 4. Do you want to c_____e a person exactly the same as you?

_____ 5. We a_____ded Ian for having the courage to tell the truth.

II. 字彙配合 (請忽略大小寫) (40%)

(A) distress   (B) brink   (C) joyous   (D) sloppy   (E) procession

_____ 1. According to the statistics, doctors' _____ handwriting killed more than 500 patients in the country per year.

_____ 2. The old man has lived in _____ since he lost his family in the fire.

_____ 3. A wedding _____ is passing along the street.

_____ 4. It is reported that the company is on the _____ of bankruptcy.

_____ 5. The little girl sang in a _____ voice.

III. 選擇題 (20%)

_____ 1. Charles is fed up with the _____ routine of everyday life.

(A) joyous   (B) conscientious   (C) monotonous   (D) glittering

_____ 2. It took over seven years for the editorial staff to compile this _____.

(A) span   (B) brink   (C) mainland   (D) encyclopedia

_____ 3. Having regular _____ enables people to find out health problems early.

(A) checkups   (B) disciples   (C) caterpillars   (D) basses

_____ 4. During takeoff and landing, passengers' seats should be in the _____ position for safety concerns.

(A) sloppy   (B) distressed   (C) careless   (D) upright

_____ 5. Hugo suffers from _____ since he often stays up late playing video games.

(A) altitude   (B) acne   (C) glitter   (D) procession

Level 6 Test 18

Class: _____ No.: _____ Name: _____ Score: _____

I. 文意字彙 (40%)

_____ 1. It's everybody's duty to c_____e natural resources.

_____ 2. Ben read the city tour b_____e before he went on a trip there.

_____ 3. The book makes a d_____e of the government's secret funds.

_____ 4. The company decides to give the employees a raise in salary to boost their m_____e.

_____ 5. The population of the country a_____es to one million.

II. 字彙配合 (請忽略大小寫) (40%)

(A) cramp	(B) itchy	(C) marginal	(D) esteem	(E) disturbance

_____ 1. Ida doesn't like to wear woolen sweaters because they would make her feel _____.

_____ 2. Because of his contribution to the field of medicine, the scholar is held in high _____.

_____ 3. The runner didn't warm up beforehand and got a(n) _____ during the race.

_____ 4. The loud noise of the traffic causes a(n) _____ to the residents.

_____ 5. The project is of _____ interest to the investors, and thus is bound to fail.

III. 選擇題 (20%)

_____ 1. The unwise man insists on living a _____ life even though he has no money to do so.

(A) significant (B) lavish (C) supplemental (D) marginal

_____ 2. All the nations of the world will be at the conference and make every _____ to solve the climate crisis.

(A) disturbance (B) closure (C) slang (D) endeavor

_____ 3. Bill was arrested for _____ into several banks' computer systems.

(A) hacking (B) chirping (C) itching (D) esteeming

_____ 4. The farm measures more than ten _____.

(A) cavities (B) sparrows (C) acres (D) ambiguities

_____ 5. The earthquake _____ the couple of their only child.

(A) preserved (B) cramped (C) deprived (D) battered

Level 6 Test 19

Class: _____ No.: _____ Name: _____ Score: _____

I. 文意字彙 (40%)

_____ 1. The policy met with a h____l of criticism. Many people complained about the inconvenience it had brought about.

_____ 2. Even though Bob transferred to his new school a week ago, he has made good a_____n to the new environment.

_____ 3. Don't d_____l on your past. It is no use thinking too much about it.

_____ 4. The task is a challenge for an expert, not to mention for a l_____n like me.

_____ 5. The huge c_____r was caused by the explosion.

II. 字彙配合 (請忽略大小寫) (40%)

(A) discreet　　(B) broil　　(C) beautify　　(D) spiral　　(E) commonplace

_____ 1. Be careful when you walk down the _____ staircase.

_____ 2. Ophelia is a _____ person. She always plans everything down to the smallest detail.

_____ 3. Mr. Robinson used to _____ a fish as the main dish for dinner.

_____ 4. Our tour guide reminds us pickpocketing is _____ in this tourist attraction.

_____ 5. Do you agree that music can _____ your mind?

III. 選擇題 (20%)

_____ 1. The _____ unit of India is the rupee.

　　(A) monetary　　(B) indiscreet　　(C) provincial　　(D) spiral

_____ 2. Thousands of civilians were _____ in this war.

　　(A) slaughtered　　(B) beautified　　(C) amplified　　(D) intensified

_____ 3. Classical music is Warren's only _____ after a bad day at school.

　　(A) coalition　　(B) ascent　　(C) expert　　(D) consolation

_____ 4. The nervous passenger sat still and kept quiet during the plane's _____.

　　(A) archaeology　　(B) nationalism　　(C) descent　　(D) celery

_____ 5. The scandal _____ people's anger at corruption.

　　(A) swarmed　　(B) kindled　　(C) grilled　　(D) enrolled

Level 6 Test 20

Class: _____ No.: _____ Name: _____ Score: _____

I. 文意字彙 (40%)

_____ 1. Everyone should be alert to this matter of great u____y.

_____ 2. We don't want a l____y explanation. Just try to briefly describe it in five minutes.

_____ 3. We tried to c____e Vicky after she broke up with her boyfriend, but in vain.

_____ 4. People d____e that woman for often stealing money from others.

_____ 5. Mom bought some pretty t____es with different patterns on them to decorate the room.

II. 字彙配合 (請忽略大小寫) (40%)

(A) heroin	(B) notable	(C) analogy	(D) escort	(E) radiant

_____ 1. The restaurant is _____ for its creamy tomato pasta.

_____ 2. The criminal was sent to jail under _____.

_____ 3. The drug dealer was caught selling _____ to the addict.

_____ 4. The speaker drew a(n) _____ between the two things and pointed out that they had many similar traits.

_____ 5. The girl with a(n) _____ smile was the center of attention.

III. 選擇題 (20%)

_____ 1. A charity is raising funds to help people living in the _____.

    (A) crocodiles   (B) radiants   (C) slums   (D) analogies

_____ 2. The principal _____ the affairs of the school.

    (A) escorts   (B) administers   (C) disgraces   (D) beeps

_____ 3. Our company provides clients with _____ training courses.

    (A) literal   (B) edible   (C) cellular   (D) comprehensive

_____ 4. The travelers were astonished at the views of Taiwan's eastern _____.

    (A) brook   (B) archive   (C) coastline   (D) heroin

_____ 5. The poor man died of _____ wounds during the war.

    (A) notable   (B) mortal   (C) stationary   (D) medieval

Level 6 Test 21

Class: _____ No.: _____ Name: _____ Score: _____

I. 文意字彙 (40%)

_____ 1. Julia ran out of her house in d_____y when the big earthquake suddenly occurred.

_____ 2. It takes perseverance to accomplish such a f_____e task.

_____ 3. Some people believe that certain herbs can help p_____y the blood.

_____ 4. An emperor has absolute s_____y over his people. Everyone has to listen to him.

_____ 5. Some students fell asleep during the long and t_____e speech.

II. 字彙配合 (請忽略大小寫) (40%)

(A) violinist	(B) perishable	(C) isle	(D) indignant	(E) shabby

_____ 1. We spent our vacation on a tropical _____.

_____ 2. Tina was _____ about being discriminated by her colleagues and called them racists.

_____ 3. Milk and meat are _____ foods so you should store them in the refrigerator.

_____ 4. A beggar in _____ clothes begged for money on the street.

_____ 5. The performance of the _____ in the concert was very impressive.

III. 選擇題 (20%)

_____ 1. Owen has been working so hard, and now he is in the management _____.

    (A) socialism   (B) isle   (C) indignation   (D) hierarchy

_____ 2. This energy crisis is without _____.

    (A) precedent   (B) unification   (C) competition   (D) motto

_____ 3. That _____ represents the current public opinion.

    (A) lieutenant   (B) outset   (C) editorial   (D) goalkeeper

_____ 4. Your visa is due to _____ in three days. You'd better renew it soon.

    (A) magnify   (B) expire   (C) oblige   (D) perish

_____ 5. There is a keen _____ between the two cities.

    (A) rivalry   (B) violinist   (C) reign   (D) statute

Level 6

Level 6 Test 22

Class: _____ No.: _____ Name: _____ Score: _____

I. 文意字彙 (40%)

_____ 1. The essence e_____ted from the rare plants is very expensive.

_____ 2. The politician f_____ed his opinions on the controversial issue during the debate.

_____ 3. Tony had badly hurt his knee and was l_____ping painfully.

_____ 4. The couple moved to the o_____s of the city to avoid the noise of the traffic.

_____ 5. Betty r_____med the streets looking for interesting shops.

II. 字彙配合 (請忽略大小寫) (40%)

(A) persevering   (B) shaver   (C) superstitious   (D) disposable   (E) electrician

_____ 1. The _____ is busy repairing the electric motor.

_____ 2. These plastic spoons are _____. However, I think we should use them again.

_____ 3. Sam uses a(n) _____ to shave his beard every morning.

_____ 4. Laura is very _____ and won't go out without bringing her lucky coin.

_____ 5. As long as you are _____, you can achieve your goal one day.

III. 選擇題 (20%)

_____ 1. The movie showed a group of criminals plotting to _____ a plane.
(A) industrialize   (B) divide   (C) hijack   (D) unify

_____ 2. These left-wing groups support _____ ideals.
(A) socialist   (B) persevering   (C) superstitious   (D) disposable

_____ 3. The tourists were awed by the _____ of the Grand Canyon.
(A) goodwill   (B) majesty   (C) precision   (D) electrician

_____ 4. Both countries _____ at the success of the peace talk.
(A) obsessed   (B) hijacked   (C) mounded   (D) rejoiced

_____ 5. David lives with his new wife and _____ in Singapore.
(A) shavers   (B) tokens   (C) vocations   (D) stepchildren

Level 6 Test 23

Class: _____ No.: _____ Name: _____ Score: _____

I. 文意字彙 (40%)

_____ 1. The riot was soon s_____sed by the police.

_____ 2. The rain came down in t_____ts and caused a flood.

_____ 3. Many people around the world m_____ned for Mother Teresa's death.

_____ 4. Nelson was e_____ed to general manager because of his excellent performance and management ability.

_____ 5. When my grandfather had an operation, all of my family worked in r_____ys to take care of him.

II. 字彙配合 (請忽略大小寫) (40%)

(A) stepfather	(B) janitor	(C) persistence	(D) vocational	(E) hoarse

_____ 1. Carol's _____ paid off when her company finally promoted her.

_____ 2. Kevin is my mother's second husband, which means he is my _____ in the family.

_____ 3. My neighbor used to be a _____ looking after a large office building in the city.

_____ 4. The little boy's voice became _____ because he had been shouting all day.

_____ 5. Helen studies in a _____ school, learning the skills at cooking.

III. 選擇題 (20%)

_____ 1. The new model of this mobile phone works much better than its _____.

    (A) defect   (B) stepfather   (C) shortcoming   (D) predecessor

_____ 2. Those who catch _____ diseases are advised to stay home.

    (A) vocational   (B) infectious   (C) extracurricular   (D) hoarse

_____ 3. The students _____ the cleaning jobs to keep the campus clean.

    (A) unveil   (B) forsake   (C) rotate   (D) overdo

_____ 4. The _____ of nuclear waste is a difficult problem.

    (A) disposal   (B) janitor   (C) grief   (D) persistence

_____ 5. The breeding season of _____ has begun since last week.

    (A) earthquakes   (B) liners   (C) gorillas   (D) manuscripts

Level 6

Level 6 Test 24

Class: _____ No.: _____ Name: _____ Score: _____

I. 文意字彙 (40%)

_____ 1. My mother prefers j_____e tea to oolong tea.

_____ 2. Shelly o_____d the two men's scheme for robbing a bank.

_____ 3. You should d_____e of batteries carefully, or they might pollute the environment.

_____ 4. Karen fluttered her e_____hes at me and gave me a charming smile.

_____ 5. Daniel's impressive q_____ns have won him many job interviews.

II. 字彙配合 (請忽略大小寫) (40%)

(A) maple	(B) reliance	(C) forthcoming	(D) mournful	(E) surge

_____ 1. Don't place too much _____ on your instinct. Think rationally before taking actions.

_____ 2. The leaves of _____ trees turn red in autumn.

_____ 3. A series of activities will take place in the _____ week.

_____ 4. Abby felt a _____ of jealousy when her boyfriend praised another girl.

_____ 5. The _____ howl of the stray dog made me decide to adopt it.

III. 選擇題 (20%)

_____ 1. Most of the _____ in this district are immigrants from Turkey.

    (A) vowels   (B) inhabitants   (C) rotations   (D) uprisings

_____ 2. We filled our car up with _____ before going on a road trip around Taiwan.

    (A) reliance   (B) sociology   (C) gospel   (D) petrol

_____ 3. The dinosaur is probably the most famous _____ animal.

    (A) prehistoric   (B) nearsighted   (C) homosexual   (D) mournful

_____ 4. Maria became the _____ of three girls after she married their father.

    (A) rebellion   (B) stepmother   (C) gasoline   (D) surge

_____ 5. My grandfather left his country as a(n) _____ at the age of twelve.

    (A) maple   (B) occurrence   (C) emigrant   (D) lining

Level 6 Test 25

Class: _____ No.: _____ Name: _____ Score: _____

I. 文意字彙 (40%)

_____ 1. A heap of r____h around the street corner attracted a lot of flies.

_____ 2. Mom cut the cabbage into long s____ds to make salad.

_____ 3. We ordered a cup of coffee and a glass of g____t juice without ice.

_____ 4. African Americans have combated i____e for hundreds of years.

_____ 5. The attendant u____red me along the aisle to my seat.

II. 字彙配合 (請忽略大小寫) (40%)

(A) overlapping   (B) mowed   (C) honorary   (D) wagged   (E) marred

_____ 1. The manager's reputation was _____ by the scandal.

_____ 2. The writer received a(n) _____ degree from York University.

_____ 3. Our jobs are _____. When there is a mistake, it is hard to decide who is to blame.

_____ 4. Yesterday, Tim _____ the lawns for his neighbors to earn some pocket money.

_____ 5. Seeing its master, the puppy _____ its tail excitedly.

III. 選擇題 (20%)

_____ 1. A(n) _____ is a sea creature that has eight tentacles and a soft body.

    (A) octopus   (B) strait   (C) premiere   (D) jockey

_____ 2. The doctor explained the details of _____ procedures to his assistants.

    (A) radioactive   (B) surgical   (C) reliant   (D) solemn

_____ 3. Jimmy has good _____. He can see things clearly far away.

    (A) dissent   (B) overlap   (C) eyesight   (D) petroleum

_____ 4. Linda raised lots of _____ such as chickens and geese in her backyard.

    (A) fowls   (B) scraps   (C) wags   (D) liters

_____ 5. We haven't heard of Alex since he _____ to Canada.

    (A) overlapped   (B) jockeyed   (C) spoiled   (D) emigrated

Level 6

45

Level 6 Test 26

Class: _____ No.: _____ Name: _____ Score: _____

I. 文意字彙 (40%)

_____ 1. The tires are easily worn down if you often drive on r____d ground.

_____ 2. The team decided to build a refuge for s____y dogs.

_____ 3. The climber f____ed her left arm after falling over a slippery rock.

_____ 4. The patient is recovering from a heart t____t operation.

_____ 5. We need more kitchen u____ls to cook a feast for fifty people.

II. 字彙配合 (請忽略大小寫) (40%)

(A) radish   (B) solitude   (C) factions   (D) walnuts   (E) distraction

_____ 1. A _____ is a red vegetable that is often eaten raw and has a spicy taste.

_____ 2. I enjoy the moments of _____ before a busy day begins.

_____ 3. The ingredients of this apple pie include apples, _____, flour, and butter.

_____ 4. The teacher was driven to _____ by the mischievous students.

_____ 5. The party split into two _____ due to different political views.

III. 選擇題 (20%)

_____ 1. All the students _____ when their teacher gave them a pop quiz.

   (A) presided   (B) surpassed   (C) groaned   (D) split

_____ 2. This small town is often praised for its good food and _____.

   (A) mastery   (B) hospitality   (C) overwork   (D) faction

_____ 3. Growing up in a slum, the girl is barely _____ and cannot write her own name.

   (A) literate   (B) jolly   (C) offshore   (D) inland

_____ 4. My beloved cat, Sophie, is my _____.

   (A) muse   (B) scream   (C) emigration   (D) solitude

_____ 5. These stone axes were _____ from prehistoric times.

   (A) pharmacists   (B) radishes   (C) relics   (D) shrieks

Level 6 Test 27

Class: _____   No.: _____   Name: _____   Score: _____

I. 文意字彙 (40%)

_____ 1. I have tried i____e times to contact the reporter.

_____ 2. The hole in the o____e layer was caused by pollution.

_____ 3. My brother u____red a groan when I told him to dump the garbage.

_____ 4. There has been a r____h of robberies in the neighborhood recently.

_____ 5. I fell off my bike yesterday, because a dog suddenly g____led at me.

II. 字彙配合 (請忽略大小寫) (40%)

(A) ward	(B) prestige	(C) mediator	(D) mustache	(E) pickpocket

_____ 1. My sister is good at negotiation and has the qualities to be a ____.

_____ 2. There is keen competition among students who wish to enter a university of high ____.

_____ 3. I think the actor looks more mature with a ____ on his upper lip.

_____ 4. The ____ was under arrest because he was caught stealing a tourist's wallet.

_____ 5. Please keep your voice down for there are other patients in the same ____.

III. 選擇題 (20%)

_____ 1. The family made a living by keeping ____ on the farm.

    (A) endowment   (B) Fahrenheit   (C) suspense   (D) livestock

_____ 2. Thomas likes perfumes and ____ flowers, such as roses and jasmines.

    (A) fragrant   (B) prestigious   (C) ruthless   (D) reckless

_____ 3. The retired couple planted evergreen ____ in their garden.

    (A) treasuries   (B) shrubs   (C) junctions   (D) wards

_____ 4. My roommate was ____ for COVID-19 last night.

    (A) strolled   (B) hospitalized   (C) diverted   (D) mediated

_____ 5. The emperor has the ____ power in his empire.

    (A) functional   (B) inoperative   (C) sovereign   (D) reminiscent

Level 6 Test 28

Class: _____ No.: _____ Name: _____ Score: _____

I. 文意字彙 (40%)

_____ 1. Stop g_____ling about your job. I don't think you can find a job better than this one.

_____ 2. The coffee tasted bitter, so Bob asked the waiter to bring him a p_____t of sugar.

_____ 3. The magician's performance is s_____g. I am impressed by it.

_____ 4. The v_____e will be given to medical and nursing staff in the hospital first.

_____ 5. Oliver tends to stay at h_____ls instead of luxurious hotels while traveling abroad.

II. 字彙配合 (請忽略大小寫) (40%)

(A) trifles	(B) lockers	(C) reptiles	(D) pilgrim	(E) endurance

_____ 1. Snakes and lizards are _____.

_____ 2. Don't waste your time on _____. You should work on more important things.

_____ 3. Swimming across the strait requires great _____.

_____ 4. We keep our clothes in the _____ when we go swimming in the pool.

_____ 5. A(n) _____ is a person who travels, usually over a long distance, for a religious purpose.

III. 選擇題 (20%)

_____ 1. The soldier stood to attention and _____ an officer.
(A) shuffled　(B) trifled　(C) saluted　(D) freaked

_____ 2. The old temple we visited in Cambodia was a great _____.
(A) weirdo　(B) reptile　(C) locker　(D) spectacle

_____ 3. My faith in artificial intelligence never _____.
(A) faltered　(B) meditated　(C) ratified　(D) privatized

_____ 4. The suspect remained _____ about the charges against her.
(A) oppressive　(B) mute　(C) insistent　(D) freak

_____ 5. There are many mosquitoes in _____.
(A) dividends　(B) warrants　(C) pilgrims　(D) swamps

Level 6 Test 29

Class: _____ No.: _____ Name: _____ Score: _____

I. 文意字彙 (40%)

_____ 1. Mom closed the s_____rs to keep out the strong sunlight.

_____ 2. Driven by v_____y, my cousin bought that sports car.

_____ 3. What can we do to e_____e the company's reputation?

_____ 4. I was deep in m_____n when the phone rang.

_____ 5. When the driver saw another car coming straight toward him, his

i_____e reaction was to turn to the right side.

II. 字彙配合 (請忽略大小寫) (40%)

(A) lodging	(B) nagging	(C) hovering	(D) warranty	(E) stutter

_____ 1. A hawk is _____ over the dying deer.

_____ 2. The school dormitory charges high for board and _____.

_____ 3. Some parents are always _____ their children to do their homework.

_____ 4. The student was so nervous that he replied with a _____.

_____ 5. This laptop computer comes with a year's _____.

III. 選擇題 (20%)

_____ 1. Architects are trying to restore the old cathedral to its original _____.

    (A) doom   (B) splendor   (C) oppression   (D) prohibition

_____ 2. The rugged terrain _____ rescue efforts.

    (A) hovered   (B) salvaged   (C) hampered   (D) stammered

_____ 3. Mexico is crossed by the _____ of Cancer.

    (A) Symmetry   (B) Tropic   (C) Warranty   (D) Familiarity

_____ 4. The chef put a _____ of salt in the soup and tasted it.

    (A) freeway   (B) lodge   (C) pinch   (D) stutter

_____ 5. The old farmer hired some young men to help him _____ the crops.

    (A) reap   (B) resent   (C) paddle   (D) hinder

Level 6

Level 6 Test 30

Class: _____ No.: _____ Name: _____ Score: _____

I. 文意字彙 (40%)

_____ 1. Knowing that my uncle is always late, I don't r_____n on his arriving on time today.

_____ 2. I felt h_____d when my classmate called me a good-for-nothing in public.

_____ 3. This power generator is p_____led by water.

_____ 4. We s_____e with the earthquake victims.

_____ 5. A d_____y is a large building at college or university where students live.

II. 字彙配合 (請忽略大小寫) (40%)

(A) feasible	(B) ordeal	(C) savage	(D) vapor	(E) waterproof

_____ 1. The poor little girl was attacked by a(n) _____ dog.

_____ 2. When water boils, it turns to _____.

_____ 3. I don't think this plan is _____. It costs too much money to put the plan into practice.

_____ 4. The boy stayed calm throughout the _____ of being kidnapped and tried to find a way to escape.

_____ 5. My coat is _____ so I can wear it outdoors in rainy days.

III. 選擇題 (20%)

_____ 1. Rick didn't want to be _____ by poor English, so he hired a tutor.
   (A) handicapped　　(B) narrated　　(C) enlightened　　(D) related

_____ 2. You can find a variety of _____ designer handbags in that shop.
   (A) lofty　　(B) feasible　　(C) mild　　(D) stylish

_____ 3. My boyfriend sometimes sinks into deep _____.
   (A) friction　　(B) melancholy　　(C) paperback　　(D) vapor

_____ 4. Two _____ are fighting outside the pub.
   (A) lads　　(B) ordeals　　(C) intakes　　(D) obstacles

_____ 5. The company's _____ denied these rumors at the press conference.
   (A) trout　　(B) plague　　(C) spokesperson　　(D) restoration

Level 6 Test 31

Class: _____ No.: _____ Name: _____ Score: _____

I. 文意字彙 (40%)

_____ 1. The patient grew too f____e to say anything.

_____ 2. Car exhaust f____es cause heavy air pollution in big cities.

_____ 3. Don't h____h your back. Stand up straight!

_____ 4. Anyone who violates the law will be p____ed.

_____ 5. If you go to bed early, you won't d____e off all the time.

II. 字彙配合 (請忽略大小寫) (40%)

(A) velvet	(B) logo	(C) mentality	(D) scraped	(E) paralyzed

_____ 1. The _____ of McDonald's two arches in bright yellow has become world-famous.

_____ 2. The driver _____ the snow off the car windows.

_____ 3. That man has the get-rich-quick _____ and doesn't know the value of hard work.

_____ 4. The car accident _____ traffic on the freeway.

_____ 5. You look pretty in black _____.

III. 選擇題 (20%)

_____ 1. The _____ promised to fix the toilet before we move in.

(A) handicraft   (B) wharf   (C) landlady   (D) logo

_____ 2. Cynthia works as a(n) _____ interpreter, which means she interprets what a speaker says in real time.

(A) orderly   (B) simultaneous   (C) subordinate   (D) secondary

_____ 3. Gloria is impressed with Tchaikovsky's *Sixth* _____.

(A) *Narrator*   (B) *Symphony*   (C) *Velvet*   (D) *Trustee*

_____ 4. The manager tried to _____ the workload among the staff members.

(A) scrape   (B) restrain   (C) reconcile   (D) equalize

_____ 5. In the past, many African people were forced to work on _____.

(A) plantations   (B) sportsmen   (C) interpreters   (D) mentalities

Level 6

Level 6 Test 32

Class: _____ No.: _____ Name: _____ Score: _____

I. 文意字彙 (40%)

_____ 1. Don't e____e the mistake with failure. If you fix it in time, you still can succeed.

_____ 2. The boy spoke in a high, f____e voice, imitating his sister.

_____ 3. We need an o____r to make arrangements for the party.

_____ 4. A car crashed into another at the i____n of the two main roads.

_____ 5. The tennis player, who always accepts victory or defeat graciously, has won praise for his good s____p.

II. 字彙配合 (請忽略大小寫) (40%)

(A) tucked	(B) skimmed	(C) subscribed	(D) mermaid	(E) veterinarian

_____ 1. A _____ is a legendary creature with a woman's upper body and a fish's tail.

_____ 2. Sam _____ his shirt into his trousers.

_____ 3. A _____ is a person who is skilled in treating animal diseases and injuries.

_____ 4. The professor _____ the pages to find the main ideas in the report.

_____ 5. I _____ to several magazines, and it cost me a lot of money.

III. 選擇題 (20%)

_____ 1. These concrete walls are built to prevent _____.

(A) landslides (B) mermaids (C) obstacles (D) veterinarians

_____ 2. When was the Suez Canal first opened for _____?

(A) restraint (B) syrup (C) navigation (D) fury

_____ 3. The thief _____ the fence with a police officer chasing after him.

(A) tucked (B) harassed (C) scanned (D) hurdled

_____ 4. Amy _____ down to find more information about the website.

(A) scrolled (B) subscribed (C) skimmed (D) plowed

5. John likes to mix _____ with soda.

(A) parliament (B) whiskey (C) redundancy (D) harassment

Level 6 Test 33

Class: _____ No.: _____ Name: _____ Score: _____

I. 文意字彙 (40%)

_____ 1. The boat struck a r_____f and began to sink.

_____ 2. When I scolded my son, he shouted back and made a sharp r_____t.

_____ 3. Judy went to Paris on the s_____r of the moment. She didn't plan it beforehand.

_____ 4. The villagers were e_____ed from their homes after a flood.

_____ 5. The teacher h_____ned his heart when dealing with his naughty students.

II. 字彙配合 (請忽略大小寫) (40%)

(A) tan	(B) turmoil	(C) hypocrite	(D) migrants	(E) latitudes

_____ 1. The plant can only be found at high _____. It doesn't grow in warm weather.

_____ 2. There are a lot of _____ looking for jobs in this big city.

_____ 3. I got a _____ after my vacation at the beach.

_____ 4. My mind was in such a _____ that I didn't know what I was saying.

_____ 5. That man is such a _____ that he praises his girlfriend to her face but speaks ill of her behind her back.

III. 選擇題 (20%)

_____ 1. Reading is Elizabeth's favorite _____.

    (A) hypocrite   (B) pastime   (C) fiancé   (D) proverb

_____ 2. Open the bottom drawer of the _____, and you will find the black shirt.

    (A) latitude   (B) dresser   (C) pony   (D) fuse

_____ 3. A medical report shows that 65% of schoolchildren in the country are _____.

    (A) orthodox   (B) wholesale   (C) migrant   (D) nearsighted

_____ 4. The government decided to _____ two billion dollars from the national budget.

    (A) intervene   (B) tan   (C) veto   (D) slash

_____ 5. The current position of the hurricane is at 81 degrees west _____ and 27 degrees north latitude.

    (A) scrutiny   (B) turmoil   (C) longitude   (D) sincerity

Level 6 Test 34

Class: _____ No.: _____ Name: _____ Score: _____

I. 文意字彙 (40%)

_____ 1. Which d_____g would you like? Caesar, Italian, or Thousand Island?

_____ 2. The lady liked the l_____t of the apartment and signed the lease immediately.

_____ 3. Calm down. Why are you making such a f_____s about that?

_____ 4. An i_____g is a huge mass of frozen ice in the sea.

_____ 5. The windows v_____ed when a strong wind blew.

II. 字彙配合 (請忽略大小寫) (40%)

(A) lotion	(B) twilight	(C) succession	(D) wholesome	(E) miscellaneous

_____ 1. At the garage sale, you can find _____ used household items sold at very low prices.

_____ 2. What you need is fresh, healthy, and _____ food.

_____ 3. A _____ of defeats discouraged the athlete from moving forward.

_____ 4. The professor devoted his _____ years to the education of the deaf.

_____ 5. This _____ keeps the moisture of your skin and makes you look young.

III. 選擇題 (20%)

_____ 1. The bluesman played the guitar and the _____.

(A) harmonica (B) evergreen (C) seagull (D) revelation

_____ 2. Bangladesh is a densely _____ country.

(A) stabilized (B) populated (C) refereed (D) slain

_____ 3. A fish moves and keeps its balance with its _____.

(A) fins (B) nostrils (C) lotions (D) ounces

_____ 4. The speech was incredibly _____! Many of the audience were dozing off.

(A) provisional (B) miscellaneous (C) tedious (D) patriotic

_____ 5. Among these friends, I feel great _____ with Michael.

(A) twilight (B) gull (C) succession (D) intimacy

Level 6 Test 35

Class: _____ No.: _____ Name: _____ Score: _____

I. 文意字彙 (40%)

_____ 1. Mary's neighbor became a w_____w after her husband died 10 years ago.

_____ 2. My aunt has d_____l citizenship. She holds an American and a Japanese passports at the same time.

_____ 3. We mustn't waste our f_____e resources. We should make the most of them.

_____ 4. There are many stars t_____ling in the sky at night.

_____ 5. The old man fainted and s_____ped to the floor.

II. 字彙配合 (請忽略大小寫) (40%)

(A) outing	(B) lottery	(C) stagger	(D) novice	(E) intonation

_____ 1. The man spent his last pennies on a(n) _____ ticket, hoping to win a big prize.

_____ 2. I am a(n) _____ at gardening. Would you please give me some advice on what to do with these flowers?

_____ 3. The drunk walked with a(n) _____ and accidentally fell off the bridge.

_____ 4. My family enjoyed the _____ at the beach last weekend.

_____ 5. In many languages, a rising _____ usually means a question.

III. 選擇題 (20%)

_____ 1. Recently, there seems to be a(n) _____ of miniskirts.

   (A) referendum　　(B) intonation　　(C) revival　　(D) vibration

_____ 2. Kevin watched his daughter picking up _____ at the beach.

   (A) pebbles　　(B) porters　　(C) beginners　　(D) tellers

_____ 3. This movie _____ memories of my school years.

   (A) stumbled　　(B) galloped　　(C) staggered　　(D) evoked

_____ 4. It has snowed for three _____ days.

   (A) imminent　　(B) successive　　(C) infinite　　(D) seductive

_____ 5. The lazy servant got scolded by the _____ of the house.

   (A) outing　　(B) mistress　　(C) lease　　(D) psychiatry

55

Level 6 Test 36

Class: _____ No.: _____ Name: _____ Score: _____

I. 文意字彙 (40%)

_____ 1. We decide to m_____e our kitchen and have a dishwasher installed.

_____ 2. The girl's parents told her not to open the box, but she could not help taking a p_____k inside.

_____ 3. The gas s_____ed the victims who were trapped in the house. Many of them fainted.

_____ 4. My classmate e_____ls not only in Chinese but also in English.

_____ 5. Two g_____rs who robbed the bank were caught.

II. 字彙配合 (請忽略大小寫) (40%)

(A) outlaw	(B) tempo	(C) posture	(D) dubious	(E) implicit

_____ 1. The fast _____ of city life exhausted me.

_____ 2. We were _____ about the drug's effects claimed by its producer.

_____ 3. Christians have _____ faith in God.

_____ 4. Robin Hood was no ordinary _____.

_____ 5. Lucy, a couch potato, enjoys sitting in a relaxed _____ and watching TV.

III. 選擇題 (20%)

_____ 1. With no one disagreeing, the board members made a _____ decision.

    (A) unanimous   (B) fireproof   (C) psychic   (D) cunning

_____ 2. The popular Korean boy group received a _____ welcome at the airport.

    (A) sly   (B) serene   (C) suspicious   (D) hearty

_____ 3. Engineers have _____ the program, and it works much faster now.

    (A) revived   (B) banned   (C) refined   (D) intrigued

_____ 4. Rubber is one of the _____ of Malaysia.

    (A) legislators   (B) outlaws   (C) staples   (D) postures

_____ 5. These three professors form the _____ of our research team.

    (A) tempo   (B) nucleus   (C) lotus   (D) victor

Level 6 Test 37

Class: _____ No.: _____ Name: _____ Score: _____

I. 文意字彙 (40%)

_____ 1. A lot of vegetarians feel that it's r_____g to eat meat.

_____ 2. Ted hated others to i_____e on his private affairs.

_____ 3. The o_____k for the new product is still uncertain. We are not sure yet whether it will sell well.

_____ 4. The flight attendant was arrested for s_____ling drugs.

_____ 5. Owing to the drought, thousands of people died of s_____n in Africa.

II. 字彙配合 (請忽略大小寫) (40%)

| (A) hedge | (B) suitcase | (C) monarch | (D) duration | (E) loudspeaker |

_____ 1. The people wanted to overthrow the _____ and establish a democratic government.

_____ 2. It always takes me a long time to pack a _____ before a trip.

_____ 3. When you are addressing a large audience, you may need a _____ to make yourself heard.

_____ 4. There will be no more flights for the _____ of the typhoon.

_____ 5. Gary was trimming the _____ when the phone rang.

III. 選擇題 (20%)

_____ 1. It is safer to wear a _____ jacket when you go cycling at night.

(A) disgusting　　(B) reflective　　(C) lesbian　　(D) naked

_____ 2. The poor old man's life was full of misery and _____.

(A) vitality　　(B) duration　　(C) monarchy　　(D) woe

_____ 3. The _____ tower is a landmark in the city.

(A) imposing　　(B) unconditional　　(C) pending　　(D) exempt

_____ 4. Environmental groups have raised public awareness of protecting the _____.

(A) loudspeakers　　(B) rebels　　(C) fisheries　　(D) suitcases

_____ 5. A therapist practices _____ by discussing problems with patients rather than by using drugs.

(A) vigor　　(B) gauge　　(C) sergeant　　(D) psychotherapy

Level 6 Test 38

Class: _____ No.: _____ Name: _____ Score: _____

I. 文意字彙 (40%)

_____ 1. The farmer begins his work at dawn and returns home at d____k.

_____ 2. The candidate had his campaign highly p_____ed so that more voters would pay attention to his policy.

_____ 3. I will e_____t myself to achieve my goal.

_____ 4. Never u_____e your opponent. I don't think you can defeat him easily.

_____ 5. The medicine can help l_____n the pain in your leg.

II. 字彙配合 (請忽略大小寫) (40%)

(A) sneakers　　(B) hemispheres　　(C) refreshments　　(D) nurturing　　(E) flourishing

_____ 1. If your business is _____, it is successful and prosperous.

_____ 2. The brain is divided into the left and right _____.

_____ 3. We believe both parents and schools should be responsible for _____ children's interests.

_____ 4. After two hours in the meeting, we took a short break and had some _____.

_____ 5. I gave my boyfriend a pair of black _____ as his birthday gift.

III. 選擇題 (20%)

_____ 1. The security guard _____ the robber to the ground.
(A) summoned　　(B) wrestled　　(C) thrived　　(D) flourished

_____ 2. The couple couldn't resist the _____ of dining at a Michelin three-star restaurant.
(A) outrage　　(B) poultry　　(C) glamour　　(D) inventory

_____ 3. The lost hiker was frightened by the _____ shadow of a giant oak tree.
(A) serial　　(B) lucrative　　(C) profitable　　(D) monstrous

_____ 4. This teacher's life _____ around his students.
(A) revolves　　(B) reduces　　(C) nurtures　　(D) imprisons

_____ 5. Abe and Sarah rent a seaside _____ for their honeymoon.
(A) villa　　(B) thermometer　　(C) peninsula　　(D) statesman

Level 6 Test 39

Class: _____ No.: _____ Name: _____ Score: _____

I. 文意字彙 (40%)

_____ 1. To set a good example for students, teachers should practice what they p_____h.

_____ 2. The little girl p_____fed out her cheeks and blew air into the balloon.

_____ 3. My cousin f_____ked out of high school for failing too many academic subjects.

_____ 4. Luckily, I only suffered s_____l injuries in that nasty accident.

_____ 5. Tom's h_____c deeds have become legends, well-known to the town folks.

II. 字彙配合 (請忽略大小寫) (40%)

(A) vines	(B) oases	(C) tilted	(D) refuted	(E) wrinkled

_____ 1. There are some _____ in the desert where travelers can get some water.

_____ 2. The suspect _____ the accusations against him.

_____ 3. The shirt _____ when Ms. Bond took it out of the wardrobe.

_____ 4. The cute puppy _____ its head to one side, looking at us.

_____ 5. The wall is covered with grape _____.

III. 選擇題 (20%)

_____ 1. The rescue team members received _____ medical training.

    (A) rigorous   (B) ironic   (C) sneaky   (D) moody

_____ 2. We _____ Helen away from the company by offering her a better career prospect.

    (A) tipped   (B) tilted   (C) lured   (D) glided

_____ 3. The _____ is closed for safety concerns.

    (A) vine   (B) underpass   (C) expenditure   (D) stationery

_____ 4. The dove _____ on the top of the flagpole.

    (A) wrinkled   (B) perched   (C) refuted   (D) dwarfed

_____ 5. The priest had a heart attack while he was preaching a(n) _____.

    (A) incline   (B) crease   (C) oasis   (D) sermon

Level 6

Level 6 Test 40

Class: _____ No.: _____ Name: _____ Score: _____

I. 文意字彙 (40%)

_____ 1. The photographer z_____med in on the model's face to take a picture.

_____ 2. I couldn't sleep well last night because someone s_____ed very loudly in the next room.

_____ 3. Tell me the e_____n date on your membership card.

_____ 4. I walked on t_____e to avoid making any noise.

_____ 5. My father is always p_____l for work; he is never late.

II. 字彙配合 (請忽略大小寫) (40%)

(A) madam	(B) oatmeal	(C) setback	(D) gloom	(E) motherhood

_____ 1. There has been a sense of _____ in the family since their pet was gone.

_____ 2. Before you decide to have a baby, make sure that you are ready for _____.

_____ 3. The politician suffered a(n) _____ in his political career and decided to give up his post.

_____ 4. May I bring you something to drink, _____?

_____ 5. Helen can make very delicious _____ cookies.

III. 選擇題 (20%)

_____ 1. The two chip manufacturers joined together to fight their common _____.

    (A) height   (B) gloom   (C) heterosexual   (D) foe

_____ 2. Alan's short _____ prevented him from becoming a fashion model.

    (A) motherhood   (B) stature   (C) priority   (D) oatmeal

_____ 3. Icy roads are very _____ to pedestrians.

    (A) bad-tempered   (B) liable   (C) perilous   (D) irritable

_____ 4. This movie _____ the wrath of the public because of its controversial content.

    (A) incurred   (B) rehabilitated   (C) preceded   (D) yearned

_____ 5. Barbara's _____ produces 600 gallons of wine every year.

    (A) madam   (B) vineyard   (C) ripple   (D) superintendent

PLUS Test 1

Class: _____ No.: _____ Name: _____ Score: _____

I. 文意字彙 (40%)

_____ 1. The little boy walked b____t in the stream.

_____ 2. Kelly's husband has a romantic s____k in him.

_____ 3. I will forgive you this time, but h____r you must not make the same mistake.

_____ 4. We will use legal and n____t means to protest against the reform.

_____ 5. My mother is always f____ting about whether I can pass the entrance exam.

II. 字彙配合 (請忽略大小寫) (40%)

(A) upheld   (B) dissuaded   (C) retaliation   (D) trot   (E) expelled

_____ 1. The traveler was walking at a steady _____.

_____ 2. The politician was _____ from his party for the bribery scandal.

_____ 3. The president claimed that the military attack was initiated not in _____ but out of a wish to administer justice.

_____ 4. David's father _____ him from studying abroad.

_____ 5. The new tax policy was not _____ by the public.

III. 選擇題 (20%)

_____ 1. These pipes are plated with _____ to stop them from rusting.

     (A) zinc   (B) trot   (C) chatter   (D) retaliation

_____ 2. The scolded child _____ her teeth to hold back the tears.

     (A) deterred   (B) clenched   (C) worried   (D) dissuaded

_____ 3. You can try to _____ the redundant words from this article.

     (A) uphold   (B) revenge   (C) grasp   (D) prune

_____ 4. Sandy's cat is sleeping on the _____.

     (A) storm   (B) hairstyle   (C) doorstep   (D) ebb

_____ 5. Many car accidents happened along the _____ road.

     (A) triumphant   (B) incidental   (C) crooked   (D) ace

PLUS

PLUS Test 2

Class: _____ No.: _____ Name: _____ Score: _____

I. 文意字彙 (40%)

_____ 1. The angry mother gave her daughter a s____k on the bottom.

_____ 2. Jason's face was d_____ted with pain when he was stung by a bee.

_____ 3. Alice went into e_____sies over her winning the lottery.

_____ 4. When something is d____t, there is not enough of it.

_____ 5. To win the final, all the players performed to the u____t of their ability.

II. 字彙配合 (請忽略大小寫) (40%)

(A) quarrelsome	(B) stump	(C) arctic	(D) thrifty	(E) expertise

_____ 1. The hiker sat on a tree _____ to take a rest.

_____ 2. We were amazed at Linda's _____ in data analysis.

_____ 3. When Leo gets drunk, he tends to become _____.

_____ 4. My husband is a(n) _____ shopper; he never buys things he doesn't need.

_____ 5. The scientist found new species of plants in _____ regions.

III. 選擇題 (20%)

_____ 1. During the winter vacation, Sylvia worked part-time at the _____ in a supermarket.

    (A) shelter   (B) expertise   (C) checkout   (D) umpire

_____ 2. The pile of tires _____ over onto the ground.

    (A) generalized   (B) toppled   (C) concluded   (D) commenced

_____ 3. The ferryman used a pair of _____ to row the boat.

    (A) oars   (B) rubies   (C) stumps   (D) reels

_____ 4. Mrs. White had _____ taste in clothes.

    (A) quarrelsome   (B) inclined   (C) argumentative   (D) exquisite

_____ 5. A North Korean athlete asked for political _____ while attending the Olympic Games.

    (A) asylum   (B) talent   (C) carbohydrate   (D) barometer

PLUS Test 3

Class: _____ No.: _____ Name: _____ Score: _____

I. 文意字彙 (40%)

_____ 1. Sam complained that his head was t_____bing with pain.

_____ 2. My fellow researchers raised a few q_____ries about my new theory.

_____ 3. Our guide took h_____d of the warning signs along the mountain path.

_____ 4. The two chess players tried hard to o_____o each other in the match.

_____ 5. The girl's shyness and fear is u_____e. She is new to our school.

II. 字彙配合 (請忽略大小寫) (40%)

(A) distrust	(B) fad	(C) clutched	(D) besieged	(E) glistened

_____ 1. The movie star was _____ by reporters as soon as she walked out of her hotel.

_____ 2. Wearing bell-bottoms was once a _____ among young people.

_____ 3. My niece _____ at my sleeve for fear that she might get lost in the crowd.

_____ 4. The dew on the leaves _____ in the sunshine.

_____ 5. Mrs. Green has a deep _____ of the Internet.

III. 選擇題 (20%)

_____ 1. The environment was _____ by severe air pollution.
   (A) degraded   (B) neglected   (C) pierced   (D) clutched

_____ 2. The delivery trucks _____ along the highway.
   (A) besieged   (B) smothered   (C) beckoned   (D) rumbled

_____ 3. The busy farmers walked across the paddy fields at a _____ pace.
   (A) valiant   (B) brisk   (C) brave   (D) mellow

_____ 4. That country is experiencing a terrible _____ as a result of climate change.
   (A) clan   (B) distrust   (C) fashion   (D) famine

_____ 5. Henry performed a(n) _____ at the Christmas party.
   (A) answer   (B) elite   (C) stunt   (D) safeguard

PLUS

PLUS Test 4

Class: _____ No.: _____ Name: _____ Score: _____

I. 文意字彙 (40%)

_____ 1. Since there was no bridge, we had to w_____e across the river.

_____ 2. The cowboy gently c_____sed the back of his horse to calm it down

_____ 3. My lawyer questioned the v_____y of the contract because I was forced to sign it.

_____ 4. The explorers g_____ed their way in the dark cave.

_____ 5. The recommended d_____e of this drug is ten milligrams a day.

II. 字彙配合 (請忽略大小寫) (40%)

(A) tranquilizers	(B) militant	(C) hysterical	(D) tariffs	(E) heralds

_____ 1. Daffodils are generally considered to be the _____ of spring.

_____ 2. The widow became _____ when someone mentioned her dead husband.

_____ 3. The senator suggested that _____ on imported goods be reduced.

_____ 4. After taking some _____, Daniel felt sleepy and went to bed.

_____ 5. The _____ workers threatened to burn down the factory if the employer refused to pay more.

III. 選擇題 (20%)

_____ 1. Since the main generator was broken, we had no choice but to use the _____ one.

    (A) hysterical   (B) auxiliary   (C) dreary   (D) barren

_____ 2. Several towns formed a _____ to develop regional trade.

    (A) blaze   (B) rustle   (C) federation   (D) tranquilizer

_____ 3. The silkworm came out of its _____ and became a moth.

    (A) ransom   (B) tariff   (C) cocoon   (D) market

_____ 4. The merchants were bargaining for spices in the _____.

    (A) bazaar   (B) trap   (C) salvation   (D) herald

_____ 5. My temper _____ up when Jason insulted my brother.

    (A) denounced   (B) overslept   (C) shunned   (D) flared

PLUS Test 5

Class: _____ No.: _____ Name: _____ Score: _____

I. 文意字彙 (40%)

_____ 1. Mary's misfortune brought her to the v___e of nervous breakdown.

_____ 2. William used a c_____l of rope to tie the newspapers.

_____ 3. I saw some birds p_____king at our fruit in the orchard.

_____ 4. The hunter waited in a_____h, attempting to shoot the bear.

_____ 5. The old lady burns i_____e to worship the goddess of mercy every day.

II. 字彙配合 (請忽略大小寫) (40%)

(A) hardy	(B) rhythmic	(C) ravaged	(D) flicked	(E) fiddled

_____ 1. Only _____ plants can survive in the desert.

_____ 2. A typhoon _____ the small town and left many people homeless.

_____ 3. I know the little girl is sleeping soundly by her _____ breathing.

_____ 4. The nervous applicant _____ with his necktie while talking with the interviewer.

_____ 5. The old man _____ away the dust on the bench and sat down.

III. 選擇題 (20%)

_____ 1. The drunken man _____ at the police officer's warning.

    (A) fiddled   (B) blundered   (C) ruined   (D) sneered

_____ 2. The drug dealers should feel ashamed of their _____ behavior.

    (A) disgraceful   (B) strong   (C) rhythmic   (D) rhetorical

_____ 3. The passengers were stuck at the airport for two days because of the _____.

    (A) saloon   (B) blizzard   (C) violin   (D) charcoal

_____ 4. The _____ writer was put in jail for her criticism of the government.

    (A) tart   (B) dissident   (C) shameful   (D) hardy

_____ 5. This pig farm is a public _____ to the neighborhood.

    (A) tread   (B) snowstorm   (C) nuisance   (D) wail

PLUS

PLUS Test 6

Class: _____ No.: _____ Name: _____ Score: _____

I. 文意字彙 (40%)

_____ 1. Most tourists are interested in the traditional r_____es that are performed by the local residents.

_____ 2. Lisa is a p_____s Catholic. She regularly donates money to the church.

_____ 3. There was a t_____r in the defendant's voice when he answered the prosecutor's question.

_____ 4. The university c_____red an honorary doctor's degree on the famous entrepreneur.

_____ 5. The major d_____k to living in the countryside is the lack of public transportation.

II. 字彙配合 (請忽略大小寫) (40%)

(A) sprawled	(B) whirl	(C) chuckled	(D) flicker	(E) pesticide

_____ 1. The murderer didn't even show a _____ of regret in front of the victim's family.

_____ 2. People use _____ to kill insects such as ants, flies, and cockroaches.

_____ 3. My mind was in a _____ after I heard the news of my son's death.

_____ 4. After a long, hard day, Jenny _____ on the bed and fell asleep quickly.

_____ 5. Frank's colleagues _____ when they saw his new hairstyle.

III. 選擇題 (20%)

_____ 1. News reporters _____ the mayor with questions about his scandal.

    (A) embarked   (B) rotated   (C) bombarded   (D) chuckled

_____ 2. Bring the soup to a _____ first and add some salt and pepper.

    (A) defect   (B) simmer   (C) pesticide   (D) giggle

_____ 3. This valley was made a wildlife _____ last month.

    (A) taunt   (B) ceremony   (C) flicker   (D) sanctuary

_____ 4. Many workers dislike the _____ project manager.

    (A) humanitarian   (B) conceited   (C) inward   (D) amiable

_____ 5. My cousin _____ bagels on the streets every day.

    (A) peddles   (B) victimizes   (C) sprawls   (D) flaps

PLUS Test 7

Class: _____ No.: _____ Name: _____ Score: _____

I. 文意字彙 (40%)

_____ 1. Andy often speaks with a s_____r when he is under stress.

_____ 2. After a shower, Stephanie b_____ded her hair carefully.

_____ 3. James paid for his new laptop by monthly i_____ts.

_____ 4. Well, I am really d_____d with your comment on my fiancée.

_____ 5. The boss obviously thought my idea was stupid because he s_____ted at whatever I said.

II. 字彙配合 (請忽略大小寫) (40%)

(A) whisked	(B) enactment	(C) relish	(D) foil	(E) terminated

_____ 1. The _____ of the new law took several months.

_____ 2. Our partnership with the local government _____ last month.

_____ 3. Wrap the sausages in _____ and heat them for five minutes.

_____ 4. The guests ate the lavish foods with _____ at the wedding.

_____ 5. The baker _____ the flies away from the apple pie.

III. 選擇題 (20%)

_____ 1. The girl _____ her doll down on the bed and stamped out of her bedroom.

(A) flung (B) imagined (C) jeered (D) whisked

_____ 2. Can you _____ what the world will be like in twenty years?

(A) terminate (B) devalue (C) visualize (D) trespass

_____ 3. My daughter had a _____ with the flu last weekend.

(A) foil (B) tale (C) bout (D) peg

_____ 4. What is the major _____ of this face cream?

(A) clamp (B) constituent (C) mockery (D) enactment

_____ 5. Martin has become an object of _____ among his peers because of his bad breath.

(A) enjoyment (B) legislation (C) relish (D) ridicule

PLUS Test 8

Class: _____ No.: _____ Name: _____ Score: _____

I. 文意字彙 (40%)

_____ 1. Helen sworn that if she found out who spread the rumor, she would w____g his neck.

_____ 2. The manager didn't like Paul and showed complete d____d for his proposal.

_____ 3. Do you think I will accept such a l____e excuse again?

_____ 4. Our host poured water into a large brass kettle to b____w tea for us.

_____ 5. If it weren't for your s____t defense, the enemy would have taken the city.

II. 字彙配合 (請忽略大小寫) (40%)

(A) designated	(B) enclosure	(C) toiled	(D) contemplation	(E) flutter

_____ 1. The lady stared at the tombstone and seemed to be lost in _____.

_____ 2. I received a letter with a(n) _____ of an application form.

_____ 3. Mr. Dowson has been _____ as the new principal.

_____ 4. Vanessa was in a(n) _____ before her debut performance.

_____ 5. The slaves _____ day and night to build the emperor's palace.

III. 選擇題 (20%)

_____ 1. The jazz musician _____ at the strings of the double bass.

    (A) ignored   (B) plucked   (C) mourned   (D) gobbled

_____ 2. The _____ army celebrated its victory in the city square.

    (A) skinny   (B) disabled   (C) repressed   (D) triumphant

_____ 3. Louisa lost her diamond _____ at the dinner party.

    (A) brooch   (B) flutter   (C) antenna   (D) plight

_____ 4. This dance music was in _____ in the 1990s.

    (A) vogue   (B) irritation   (C) reflection   (D) toil

_____ 5. The fugitive _____ behind the fence in order to hide himself.

    (A) sprinted   (B) lamented   (C) crouched   (D) designated

PLUS Test 9

Class: _____ No.: _____ Name: _____ Score: _____

I. 文意字彙 (40%)

_____ 1. Richard u_____ked his suitcases as soon as he got home from the airport.

_____ 2. My sons g_____ed themselves on hamburgers at McDonald's.

_____ 3. Professor Chen displayed great i_____y in designing this drone.

_____ 4. These rocks have been steadily e_____ed away by the river.

_____ 5. After the peace talk, both countries signed a p_____t to officially end the war.

II. 字彙配合 (請忽略大小寫) (40%)

(A) lyrics	(B) sewers	(C) vulgar	(D) cordial	(E) picturesque

_____ 1. When Joe opened the door, he marveled at the _____ view of the terraced rice fields.

_____ 2. Alice was provoked by the host's _____ jokes and slapped him in the face.

_____ 3. On my first day to the office, my colleagues gave me a _____ welcome.

_____ 4. The _____ around this chemical plant give off nasty smells.

_____ 5. The instructor played a French song and asked us to write down the _____ in order to test our listening comprehension.

III. 選擇題 (20%)

_____ 1. Tim sat under the free, _____ over his parent's divorce.
(A) buckling   (B) cleansing   (C) brooding   (D) foreseeing

_____ 2. The bomb technician managed to _____ the explosive device put under the governor's car.
(A) endanger   (B) dismantle   (C) tramp   (D) drizzle

_____ 3. This apple is fresh and _____.
(A) vulgar   (B) diplomatic   (C) crunchy   (D) resolute

_____ 4. It was not _____ of you to turn down the mayor's invitation.
(A) stern   (B) picturesque   (C) menacing   (D) tactful

_____ 5. Juliet keeps a mirror in her _____.
(A) pocketbook   (B) antibody   (C) treaty   (D) yarn

PLUS Test 10

Class: _____ No.: _____ Name: _____ Score: _____

I. 文意字彙 (40%)

_____ 1. It is said that Indians s_____y their agreement by shaking their head.

_____ 2. The p_____rs who kill elephants for the tusks should be condemned and punished.

_____ 3. George s_____ped down to pick up the coins under the table.

_____ 4. My advisor is e_____c about handing in the term paper on time.

_____ 5. The tourists paid the money with g_____e because they believed that they had found good bargains.

II. 字彙配合 (請忽略大小寫) (40%)

(A) recurrence	(B) dynamite	(C) brutish	(D) gulp	(E) cosmopolitan

_____ 1. Nero was a _____ ruler in ancient Rome.

_____ 2. New York is a _____ city, where you can meet people from all over the world.

_____ 3. The engineering team blew up the huge rock with tons of _____.

_____ 4. The _____ of the same mistake is completely unacceptable.

_____ 5. The hungry diner swallowed the bacon in one _____.

III. 選擇題 (20%)

_____ 1. We haven't seen Ted for a long time since he _____ to Barcelona.
    (A) recurred   (B) darted   (C) resisted   (D) migrated

_____ 2. This paint cannot _____ high temperatures.
    (A) prop   (B) withstand   (C) simmer   (D) swallow

_____ 3. Ron is a biologist. He has stored a lot of specimens in the _____.
    (A) temperament   (B) cellar   (C) artery   (D) explosive

_____ 4. The mayor _____ the president's position, but she never made it.
    (A) coveted   (B) dispatched   (C) trampled   (D) gulped

_____ 5. A plan of such _____ will take at least one year to complete.
    (A) dynamite   (B) yeast   (C) magnitude   (D) materialism

進階英文字彙力
4501～6000PLUS
習題本

Answer Key

Level 5–2 Test 1
I. 1. briefcase　2. exterior　3. entitled
　　4. republican　5. trimmed
II. 1. C　2. D　3. E　4. B　5. A
III.1. B　2. A　3. D　4. C　5. C

Level 5–2 Test 2
I. 1. bronze　2. clustered　3. scrambled
　　4. straightened　5. fabulous
II. 1. C　2. A　3. B　4. D　5. E
III.1. C　2. B　3. D　4. A　5. D

Level 5–2 Test 3
I. 1. granted　2. patent　3. slammed
　　4. comprised　5. nominate
II. 1. B　2. E　3. A　4. C　5. D
III.1. B　2. D　3. A　4. C　5. D

Level 5–2 Test 4
I. 1. fascinated　2. tuition　3. auction
　　4. irony　5. disconnected
II. 1. D　2. E　3. C　4. B　5. A
III.1. C　2. C　3. A　4. A　5. B

Level 5–2 Test 5
I. 1. indulge　2. smashed　3. submit
　　4. raid　5. greed
II. 1. B　2. D　3. E　4. A　5. C
III.1. B　2. A　3. D　4. D　5. C

Level 5–2 Test 6
I. 1. conceived　2. democrat　3. viewpoint
　　4. metropolitan　5. resume
II. 1. B　2. D　3. A　4. E　5. C
III.1. C　2. B　3. A　4. B　5. C

Level 5–2 Test 7
I. 1. minimal　2. grill　3. retail　4. vinegar
　　5. substantial
II. 1. B　2. E　3. A　4. D　5. C
III.1. B　2. D　3. C　4. C　5. A

Level 5–2 Test 8
I. 1. erect　2. visa　3. documentary
　　4. nutrients　5. grip
II. 1. B　2. E　3. D　4. A　5. C
III.1. A　2. A　3. D　4. C　5. B

Level 5–2 Test 9
I. 1. prevailing　2. rattled　3. confession
　　4. Underline　5. observer
II. 1. E　2. C　3. D　4. B　5. A
III.1. B　2. D　3. A　4. C　5. C

Level 5–2 Test 10
I. 1. batch　2. petty　3. escalator
　　4. confined　5. supervising
II. 1. A　2. D　3. B　4. C　5. E
III.1. D　2. C　3. D　4. A　5. B

Level 5–2 Test 11
I. 1. lawmaker　2. descended　3. session
　　4. confronted　5. stacks
II. 1. B　2. D　3. E　4. A　5. C
III.1. B　2. C　3. C　4. B　5. A

Level 5–2 Test 12
I. 1. unemployment　2. despair
　　3. consensus　4. warehouse　5. league
II. 1. A　2. B　3. C　4. E　5. D
III.1. D　2. B　3. D　4. A　5. B

Level 5–2 Test 13
I. 1. stake　2. crude　3. orchard
　　4. constitutional　5. doorway
II. 1. B　2. C　3. D　4. A　5. E
III.1. C　2. B　3. A　4. C　5. C

Level 5–2 Test 14
I. 1. stall　2. fraud　3. dough　4. prone
　　5. chord
II. 1. E　2. C　3. A　4. B　5. D
III.1. D　2. B　3. C　4. A　5. B

Level 5–2 Test 15
I. 1. freighted　2. weird　3. recruit
　　4. upgraded　5. blushed
II. 1. C　2. D　3. E　4. B　5. A
III.1. C　2. D　3. D　4. A　5. B

Level 5–2 Test 16
I. 1. bolted　2. outlet　3. symptoms
　　4. whining　5. diameter
II. 1. D　2. C　3. A　4. E　5. B
III.1. B　2. D　3. B　4. A　5. C

Level 5–2 Test 17

I. 1. mumbled   2. shivered   3. integrate
   4. sparkling   5. pirates
II. 1. B   2. C   3. E   4. A   5. D
III. 1. A   2. B   3. C   4. A   5. D

Level 5–2 Test 18

I. 1. digestion   2. wilderness   3. decay
   4. overhead   5. transit
II. 1. E   2. C   3. D   4. B   5. A
III. 1. C   2. C   3. D   4. B   5. A

Level 5–2 Test 19

I. 1. exploits   2. dimensions   3. specified
   4. tempted   5. shrugged
II. 1. B   2. A   3. E   4. C   5. D
III. 1. D   2. A   3. C   4. B   5. C

Level 5–2 Test 20

I. 1. enthusiastic   2. complication
   3. mythical   4. dedicate   5. shuttle
II. 1. D   2. A   3. B   4. E   5. C
III. 1. B   2. B   3. D   4. A   5. C

Level 6 Test 1

I. 1. consonants   2. coral   3. annoyance
   4. detach   5. merchandise
II. 1. E   2. C   3. D   4. B   5. A
III. 1. D   2. C   3. B   4. D   5. A

Level 6 Test 2

I. 1. antibiotics   2. soothe   3. crutches
   4. underneath   5. blazed
II. 1. B   2. E   3. D   4. C   5. A
III. 1. A   2. D   3. C   4. B   5. B

Level 6 Test 3

I. 1. lingered   2. hygiene   3. orphanage
   4. fable   5. villain
II. 1. C   2. E   3. A   4. D   5. B
III. 1. B   2. B   3. A   4. C   5. D

Level 6 Test 4

I. 1. fragrance   2. lizard   3. excess
   4. accumulate   5. assassinated
II. 1. C   2. E   3. D   4. B   5. A
III. 1. D   2. C   3. B   4. C   5. A

Level 6 Test 5

I. 1. blot   2. apprentice   3. compile
   4. outright   5. oriental
II. 1. D   2. E   3. B   4. C   5. A
III. 1. A   2. B   3. C   4. A   5. B

Level 6 Test 6

I. 1. rehearse   2. paradox   3. devoured
   4. spotlight   5. lullaby
II. 1. B   2. D   3. A   4. E   5. C
III. 1. D   2. D   3. C   4. B   5. C

Level 6 Test 7

I. 1. complexion   2. differentiate
   3. ornamented   4. bachelor   5. fertility
II. 1. A   2. B   3. D   4. E   5. C
III. 1. A   2. C   3. B   4. B   5. D

Level 6 Test 8

I. 1. overflows   2. fertilizer   3. pimples
   4. dictation   5. compute
II. 1. A   2. B   3. C   4. D   5. E
III. 1. C   2. D   3. A   4. C   5. B

Level 6 Test 9

I. 1. fortified   2. polar   3. patriot
   4. dictator   5. computerization
II. 1. B   2. A   3. D   4. C   5. E
III. 1. B   2. C   3. A   4. C   5. D

Level 6 Test 10

I. 1. healthful   2. cholesterol   3. captivity
   4. dictatorship   5. dispensable
II. 1. E   2. A   3. D   4. B   5. C
III. 1. A   2. D   3. D   4. A   5. B

Level 6 Test 11

I. 1. permissible   2. counterparts
   3. accountable   4. playwright   5. Folklore
II. 1. B   2. E   3. A   4. D   5. C
III. 1. C   2. B   3. D   4. A   5. C

Level 6 Test 12

I. 1. screwdriver   2. refresh   3. amid
   4. inclusive   5. invaluable
II. 1. A   2. C   3. E   4. B   5. D
III. 1. B   2. B   3. A   4. A   5. D

Level 6 Test 13

I. 1. Geographically 2. chimpanzee
3. pondered 4. academy 5. condense
II. 1. B 2. E 3. D 4. A 5. C
III. 1. C 2. A 3. D 4. B 5. C

Level 6 Test 14

I. 1. Diabetes 2. Geometry 3. backbone
4. previews 5. Sanitation
II. 1. B 2. E 3. D 4. A 5. C
III. 1. B 2. B 3. D 4. C 5. A

Level 6 Test 15

I. 1. disbelief 2. lifelong 3. sculptor
4. breakup 5. casualties
II. 1. E 2. C 3. B 4. A 5. D
III. 1. D 2. C 3. A 4. A 5. B

Level 6 Test 16

I. 1. lighten 2. flaw 3. antonym
4. simplicity 5. momentum
II. 1. D 2. A 3. C 4. B 5. E
III. 1. A 2. B 3. A 4. D 5. C

Level 6 Test 17

I. 1. garments 2. disciplinary 3. crammed
4. clone 5. applauded
II. 1. D 2. A 3. E 4. B 5. C
III. 1. C 2. D 3. A 4. D 5. B

Level 6 Test 18

I. 1. conserve 2. brochure 3. disclosure
4. morale 5. approximates
II. 1. B 2. D 3. A 4. E 5. C
III. 1. B 2. D 3. A 4. C 5. C

Level 6 Test 19

I. 1. hail 2. adaptation 3. dwell
4. layman 5. crater
II. 1. D 2. A 3. B 4. E 5. C
III. 1. A 2. A 3. D 4. C 5. B

Level 6 Test 20

I. 1. urgency 2. lengthy 3. console
4. despise 5. textiles
II. 1. B 2. D 3. A 4. C 5. E
III. 1. C 2. B 3. D 4. C 5. B

Level 6 Test 21

I. 1. dismay 2. formidable 3. purify
4. superiority 5. tiresome
II. 1. C 2. D 3. B 4. E 5. A
III. 1. D 2. A 3. C 4. B 5. A

Level 6 Test 22

I. 1. extracted 2. formulated 3. limping
4. outskirts 5. roamed
II. 1. E 2. D 3. B 4. C 5. A
III. 1. C 2. A 3. B 4. D 5. D

Level 6 Test 23

I. 1. suppressed 2. torrents 3. mourned
4. elevated 5. relays
II. 1. C 2. A 3. B 4. E 5. D
III. 1. D 2. B 3. C 4. A 5. C

Level 6 Test 24

I. 1. jasmine 2. overheard 3. dispose
4. eyelashes 5. qualifications
II. 1. B 2. A 3. C 4. E 5. D
III. 1. B 2. D 3. A 4. B 5. C

Level 6 Test 25

I. 1. rubbish 2. shreds 3. grapefruit
4. injustice 5. ushered
II. 1. E 2. C 3. A 4. B 5. D
III. 1. A 2. B 3. C 4. A 5. D

Level 6 Test 26

I. 1. rugged 2. stray 3. fractured
4. transplant 5. utensils
II. 1. A 2. B 3. D 4. E 5. C
III. 1. C 2. B 3. A 4. A 5. C

Level 6 Test 27

I. 1. innumerable 2. ozone 3. uttered
4. rash 5. growled
II. 1. C 2. B 3. D 4. E 5. A
III. 1. D 2. A 3. B 4. B 5. C

Level 6 Test 28

I. 1. grumbling 2. packet 3. stunning
4. vaccine 5. hostels
II. 1. C 2. A 3. E 4. B 5. D
III. 1. C 2. D 3. A 4. B 5. D

Level 6 Test 29
I. 1. shutters   2. vanity   3. enhance
   4. meditation   5. instinctive
II. 1. C   2. A   3. B   4. E   5. D
III.1. B   2. C   3. B   4. C   5. A

Level 6 Test 30
I. 1. reckon   2. humiliated   3. propelled
   4. sympathize   5. dormitory
II. 1. C   2. D   3. A   4. B   5. E
III.1. A   2. D   3. B   4. A   5. C

Level 6 Test 31
I. 1. feeble   2. fumes   3. hunch
   4. prosecuted   5. doze
II. 1. B   2. D   3. C   4. E   5. A
III.1. C   2. B   3. B   4. D   5. A

Level 6 Test 32
I. 1. equate   2. feminine   3. organizer
   4. intersection   5. sportsmanship
II. 1. D   2. A   3. E   4. B   5. C
III.1. A   2. C   3. D   4. A   5. B

Level 6 Test 33
I. 1. reef   2. retort   3. spur   4. evacuated
   5. hardened
II. 1. E   2. D   3. A   4. B   5. C
III.1. B   2. B   3. D   4. D   5. C

Level 6 Test 34
I. 1. dressing   2. layout   3. fuss
   4. iceberg   5. vibrated
II. 1. E   2. D   3. C   4. B   5. A
III.1. A   2. B   3. A   4. C   5. D

Level 6 Test 35
I. 1. widow   2. dual   3. finite   4. twinkling
   5. slumped
II. 1. B   2. D   3. C   4. A   5. E
III.1. C   2. A   3. D   4. B   5. B

Level 6 Test 36
I. 1. modernize   2. peek   3. suffocated
   4. excels   5. gangsters
II. 1. B   2. D   3. E   4. A   5. C
III.1. A   2. D   3. C   4. C   5. B

Level 6 Test 37
I. 1. revolting   2. intrude   3. outlook
   4. smuggling   5. starvation
II. 1. C   2. B   3. E   4. D   5. A
III.1. B   2. D   3. A   4. C   5. D

Level 6 Test 38
I. 1. dusk   2. publicized   3. exert
   4. underestimate   5. lessen
II. 1. E   2. B   3. D   4. C   5. A
III.1. B   2. C   3. D   4. A   5. A

Level 6 Test 39
I. 1. preach   2. puffed   3. flunked
   4. superficial   5. heroic
II. 1. B   2. D   3. E   4. C   5. A
III.1. A   2. C   3. B   4. B   5. D

Level 6 Test 40
I. 1. zoomed   2. snored   3. expiration
   4. tiptoe   5. punctual
II. 1. D   2. E   3. C   4. A   5. B
III.1. D   2. B   3. C   4. A   5. B

PLUS Test 1
I. 1. barefoot   2. streak   3. hereafter
   4. nonviolent   5. fretting
II. 1. D   2. E   3. C   4. B   5. A
III.1. A   2. B   3. D   4. C   5. C

PLUS Test 2
I. 1. smack   2. distorted   3. ecstasies
   4. deficient   5. utmost
II. 1. B   2. E   3. A   4. D   5. C
III.1. C   2. B   3. A   4. D   5. A

PLUS Test 3
I. 1. throbbing   2. queries   3. heed
   4. outdo   5. understandable
II. 1. D   2. B   3. C   4. E   5. A
III.1. A   2. D   3. B   4. D   5. C

PLUS Test 4
I. 1. wade   2. caressed   3. validity
   4. groped   5. dosage
II. 1. E   2. C   3. D   4. A   5. B
III.1. B   2. C   3. C   4. A   5. D

PLUS Test 5

I. 1. verge　2. coil　3. pecking　4. ambush
　　5. incense
II. 1. A　2. C　3. B　4. E　5. D
III.1. D　2. A　3. B　4. B　5. C

PLUS Test 6

I. 1. rites　2. pious　3. tremor　4. conferred
　　5. drawback
II. 1. D　2. E　3. B　4. A　5. C
III.1. C　2. B　3. D　4. B　5. A

PLUS Test 7

I. 1. stammer　2. braided　3. installments
　　4. displeased　5. snorted
II. 1. B　2. E　3. D　4. C　5. A
III.1. A　2. C　3. C　4. B　5. D

PLUS Test 8

I. 1. wring　2. disregard　3. lame　4. brew
　　5. stout
II. 1. D　2. B　3. A　4. E　5. C
III.1. B　2. D　3. A　4. A　5. C

PLUS Test 9

I. 1. unpacked　2. gorged　3. ingenuity
　　4. eroded　5. pact
II. 1. E　2. C　3. D　4. B　5. A
III.1. C　2. B　3. C　4. D　5. A

PLUS Test 10

I. 1. signify　2. poachers　3. stooped
　　4. emphatic　5. glee
II. 1. C　2. E　3. B　4. A　5. D
III.1. D　2. B　3. B　4. A　5. C

20 分鐘 稱霸 大考英文作文

王靖賢　編著

- 共16回作文練習，涵蓋大考作文3大題型：看圖寫作、主題寫作、信函寫作。根據近年大考趨勢精心出題，題型多元且擬真度高。
- 每回作文練習皆有為考生精選的英文名言佳句，增強考生備考戰力。
- 附方便攜帶的解析本，針對每回作文題目提供寫作架構圖，讓寫作脈絡一目了然，並提供範文、寫作要點、寫作撇步及好用詞彙，一本在手即可增強英文作文能力。